THE ENEMY SKY

Day after day Frank Thompson's
squadron of Sopwith Pups swept across
the enemy lines, strafing, bombing, and
tangling with the German Albatros.
It was a new kind of war. The losses
of men and machines were high,
but so were their spirits.
They knew that victory was near.

A NOVEL OF THE ROYAL FLYING
CORPS

BY THE AUTHOR OF
THE UNFEELING SKY

Also by Peter Saxon

THE UNFEELING SKY

and published by Corgi Books

Peter Saxon

The Enemy Sky

CORGI BOOKS
A DIVISION OF TRANSWORLD PUBLISHERS

THE ENEMY SKY

A CORGI BOOK 552 08255 4

First publication in Great Britain

PRINTING HISTORY

Corgi edition published 1969
Copyright © Peter Saxon 1969

This book is set in Pilgrim 10 pt.

Corgi Books are published by Transworld Publishers, Ltd.
Bashley Road, London, N.W.10

Made and printed in Great Britain by
Richard Clay (The Chaucer Press), Ltd., Bungay, Suffolk

The Enemy Sky

CHAPTER ONE

The morning had a strange light. It was as though one were being reborn in another atmosphere. Frank Thompson, confident in his awareness of the machine he was flying, pushed forward surely on the control column until his airspeed had built up to a hundred and twenty-five miles per hour. The throttle was now fully open. He pulled back on the stick and exerted full left rudder and aileron. Careful when inverted, to keep the nose of the Sopwith Pup on the horizon, he allowed it to go around. And then he was out. The slow roll had cost him less than a hundred feet. It wasn't bad. Not good, but not all that bad.

It was great to be alive.

Beneath him the gently spreading folds of France lay as though nothing as ugly as war had ever touched them. It was a delightful day. When he landed, Frank decided, he would have a few words with his rigger. There wasn't much wrong with the machine, but she had a certain tendency to fly left wing down. It was not serious.

Now—and it was something Frank could not quite understand—they talked of death too much. He could not understand why, for he had been born a hunter and had grown as one. He felt no pity for the dead victim. His death was as natural as his own would be when the time came for him to die.

But now there was a cloud to play with. He turned the Pup into a steep bank to starboard, leapt at the fleecy whiteness, missed it—just—and then was in the blue again.

Wasn't it a pity that his brother could not share this delight. They had shared so much when they were boys. Harry was taking the war seriously. He was on the staff of the First Army. Perhaps Harry would make a name for himself as a soldier.

Oh God, now. Why couldn't he fall? Frank was thinking of Sarah. Now it was March 1917 and the war had become something quite different. Six months before—and he trembled as he thought about it, and of why they had sent him home.

Then he tensed his knees and relaxed his fingers on the stick. An aeroplane—and it was the first thing he had ever been taught, without really having to be taught—will fly itself. The less interference it has from the pilot, the better.

He was in the sky. It was all his. The months in England were over. The life of which he had only dreamed was over.

Sarah had written to say that after all she could not marry him. Sarah, Sarah, Sarah ... There was a suggestion of tears·reaching his eyes; and then again, almost sensually, he was aware of the machine. He had been airborne now for forty-five minutes. Below there were these people he did not know. New people. It was difficult.

Frank turned towards the airfield. If there was one thing he had to do, it was to forget Sarah.

At Uphaven, instructing the boys who were so ready to prove themselves, it had been possible for him to ride home on the Norton to Abbott's Wednesday. One weekend she had been there. He had known of her as a distant cousin. Harry had told him about her. But he had never met her until that weekend. He had loved her, and in a strange way he had given away much of himself.

Her father, the Colonel, was not unkind. In a way he had been right. Frank had nothing. What little there was in the family would go to Harry. Harry was trying to build a serious career. Frank—and he had to admit it even to himself—was a feckless aviator. There was nothing else in his life that he could imagine doing. He prayed God—and perhaps Sarah had sensed this—that he would not survive the war.

But forgetting all that now, he savoured the delight of the morning. Breakfast was waiting. The night before he had arrived, and he had decided that morning to air-test the Pup they had assigned him. He was now approaching the airfield, and he smiled to himself. From four thousand feet he would execute a dead-stick landing.

8

He was positioned; throttle back—if this engine cooled there would be no restarting it—the only sound the whispering of the wind in the wires. For him it was such a gentle sound, like his mother's voice. Now he was tensed; there was no thought of Sarah, no memory of the words he had spoken. There was only the wind against him. Losing a hundred and fifty feet a minute, he glided around the field. He picked his spot. He did more than that—he chose the exact scar on the grass where he would touch down.

Down, gently. There was nothing in the world yet stirring. Left bank, rudder, stick, down, down ... Over the fence, airspeed steady ... hold it, back. Gently ... hold it. Back into the crutch, down. He missed his spot by six yards. Fair.

Frank taxi-ed the aircraft towards the hangar and felt a strange warmth when he saw the ground-crew running towards him. When they reached him they caught hold of his plane's wing-tips. There was the odd scratching of the voices against the smell of the machine. They held the plane down and when he had cut the ignition he climbed out.

'Morning, sir!'

'Morning, Corporal.'

'Everything all right?'

'Well, almost ...'

Frank walked away from them. It was not his fashion to ingratiate himself with the ground-crew in any way. He loved them, but in his own time.

'Sir!'

Frank, who was tall and tended to droop at the shoulders, paused in his stride. As he halted and turned he saw the corporal half-running towards him.

'Sir——'

Frank waited.

'Just to say, sir, that I knew Sergeant McFee. He taught me all I knew about rigging. May I say, sir, how proud we all are to have you on the Squadron.'

Frank Thompson was embarrassed. He was aware of the fact that his record on the Western Front was as decent as any man's, considering everything.

When he was embarrassed he stammered slightly, an old childhood habit he had not quite succeeded in breaking. He stammered now, a little.

9

'Wh-where is the S-Sergeant?'

'He's still with your old Squadron, sir. As far as I know.'

'What's your name, Corporal?'

'Smithers, sir.'

'Corporal Smithers, I'm glad to meet you.'

At least here was one person who was not entirely new. Frank accepted the man's salute, then turned and continued on his way to the Mess.

Suddenly the morning had changed. There was a quick shower and as the rain hit him, Frank ran for shelter. His belly was empty and the thought of food was warming. What was worrying him, if he had faced the question then, was the thought that he had not yet met the C.O.

Major J. T. Simpson, O.B.E., had served with some minor distinction in the Boer War. His regiment had been the Sherwood Foresters, but most of the war he had been detached to a column of mounted infantry as officer in charge of mules. To be fair to the Major, he was a stolid, brave-enough man, but his mind had been locked in that earlier war. The new ways of 1914 had not been to his liking when he had been recalled from the reserve. At the earliest possible opportunity he had applied for transfer to the Royal Flying Corps; here at least there was the possibility of fresh fields to conquer.

In a way there had been. In its earlier role the R.F.C. had fulfilled the function of a kind of aerial cavalry—scouting, acting as the eyes of the artillery, executing, indeed, some very useful work for Army and Corps commanders. It had never been envisaged that men should actually try to destroy each other in the air.

Deep in his heart Major Simpson looked on aerial fighting as a negation of a Flying Corps's real purpose. Deep in his heart, too, he didn't like the business—not that he had often been involved in air combat; that was not his purpose. He was there primarily to administer the Squadron, which duty he carried out with an unbending rectitude which had earned him the nickname of 'Old Glass-Arse'.

When Frank entered the Mess dining-room there were perhaps a dozen members of the Squadron there, eating breakfast. His eyes quickly scanned the room and he could see a thick-set man in his mid-thirties sitting alone at the far end of the room. This, he assumed, must be the Major.

Frank sat at a table near the door where two other pilots were eating. He muttered a somewhat subdued 'G'morning'.

'Hi,' the first of the men to speak said. 'I'm Delaney.'

'I'm Thompson.'

'Yeah, we know.'

The other pilot, sitting on Frank's right, introduced himself as Cardew. He was a pleasant, fresh-faced young man of about twenty, undoubtedly one of the inexperienced boys who had recently been sent to France in such large numbers. He was obviously shy and conscious of Frank's evident experience.

'Are you Canadian?' Frank asked of the man who had called himself Delaney.

'Hell, no. I'm American—Newark, New Jersey, American.'

'I thought,' Frank said haltingly, 'I thought the Americans were all with the French . . .'

'Not this American, not me. I like to be where I can speak American.'

Delaney was obviously a character and Frank felt himself warm to the man. It was strange, but even with the evidence of what he had seen the previous evening and what he was seeing now, he was still experiencing that shyness he had known on his first day at prep school.

'You were airborne this morning——'

Frank's mouth was full of scrambled egg. He nodded assent.

'How do you like the Pup?'

'Well, out here. I'm a Nisuport man myself, but I don't mind the Pup. The one I flew this morning handles quite nicely.'

There was a silence then, and Frank realised that perhaps he had sounded patronising in his reference to 'out here'. He knew nothing about this Squadron, but he was beginning to have a suspicion that it was not much experienced as a Fighter Squadron. There was no real evidence of any experience on the tunics of the men around him.

His suspicion was verified when Delaney said, a shade gruffly : 'They're a goddamned sight better machines than those old blunderbusses we were using until six weeks ago.'

'The F.E. ?'

'Yeah. Goddamned deathtraps——'

Frank finished eating and lit a cigarette. 'And has the Squadron only recently reformed, then?'

'Yeah, didn't they tell you? Until six weeks ago we were the sitting ducks of reconnaissance. It's mighty refreshing to feel now that we're the boys who dispense the justice.'

Cardew spoke. He said: 'Perhaps that's why they've posted you here.'

'Why?'

'To help . . .' Cardew looked to Delaney as though for confirmation before going on '. . . to help strengthen us with your experience.'

Frank felt it best to change the subject. 'Have you seen anything of this new Fokker Triplane we've heard so much about?' he asked them both.

'We haven't,' Delaney interjected. 'But it's around. Richthofen is using one, they say, but so far we've not had the privilege of meeting the gentleman—thank God!'

Somehow, in the way these men spoke, more than that perhaps, in the whole atmosphere of the mess, there was a kind of uncertainty—almost a lack of confidence—and it was as he was thinking this that Frank was conscious of the Major walking towards him from his table at the far end. The Major stopped and Frank stood, as did the other two.

Major Simpson said: 'You're Thompson?'

'Sir.'

'Be in my office in ten minutes, Captain Thompson.'

'Sir.'

The Major strode on. He was not as tall as Frank, but thick-set and strong-looking, though not fat. There was something in the man's broad face that was vaguely disturbing, however.

As they sat down again Delaney said: 'Old Glass-arse looks as though his night in town has left him feeling rather wanting.'

'He's not so bad,' Cardew said quickly.

'Naw, you're right. He's not so bad.'

'He's a Sherwood Forester,' Frank said. The Major was still wearing the uniform of his old regiment.

'Yeah, you're right.' There was a tinge of bitterness in the American's voice. 'But if you can tell me what the hell a Sherwood Forester is doing in command of a Squadron of Sopwith Pups, you're a better man than I am.'

Frank excused himself, went to the toilet, and then asked a waiter where he might find the C.O.'s office.

It was in a wooden hut beside one of the temporary hangars that he been erected to house the aircraft. Frank knocked, entered, saluted and was invited by the Major to sit down.

'Welcome to the Squadron,' the Major said. He used the words without feeling.

'Thank you, sir.'

'Thompson, I may as well tell you now that we're in trouble. Not only this Squadron—the whole Corps is in trouble. Our aircraft as hopelessly outclassed by this new D.B.III. the Boche are using. Our pilots—and referring particularly to this Squadron—are inexperienced. Some of these boys I'm using are coming out here with something like fifteen hours' solo experience. It's criminal. I haven't time to allow them to familiarise themselves with the aircraft they're flying, let alone give them time to learn to fight the damn things——'

'Aren't the new Camels due in service soon, sir?'

'We've been promised them for months. God knows when we'll see them—if ever.'

Frank stirred restlessly.

'Five minutes ago, for instance, Wing instructed me to mount an offensive patrol—seventeen thousand five hundred feet—fifteen miles into Hunland. I want you to lead it, a Flight of four aircraft.'

'Me, sir?'

'Yes, you. Why not?'

'Sir, I—I'd be d-delighted to fly with it. B-but lead it—is that wise, sir?'

'*I'm* here to decide what's wise, Thompson.'

But Frank persisted. 'Sir, I think this is quite wrong. I don't know the men I'm flying with. They don't know me. They may not understand my signals.'

'You can have those two you were eating breakfast with —Delaney and young Cardew, with one other. There's an hour to teach them. The other will be me.'

'*You*, sir?'

'Dammit, man, why not? Don't you think I can fly?'

'Of course, sir.'

'We'll brief in fifteen minutes. That will be all, Thompson. Instruct your rigger to attach Flight Commander's ribbons to your aircraft.'

'Yes, sir.' Frank saluted and turned towards the door.

'Thompson——'

'Yes, sir?'

'This doesn't mean that you've been appointed a Flight Commander. But there is a vacancy with B Flight. It could well mean that you will be.'

An hour later the four aircraft were warming up in preparation for take-off. It was a long time since Frank Thompson had felt that particular stirring in his insides that comes to a man when he is about to take off on an offensive patrol. It isn't fear. There is too much on which to concentrate to allow oneself the luxury of fear.

Frank now checked that the aircraft on either side of him were in readiness. Young Cardew was on his port side, sitting there, somehow giving the impression of nervous eagerness. On his immediate starboard was Delaney, the American. Delaney gave him a thumbs-up sign. Frank smiled. There was a certain pride in seeing a Flight Commander's ribbons streaming out from the main braces on either wing.

He revved the rotary once more and when he had heard the engine respond smoothly, he throttled back and waved to the two airmen who held his chocks.

'Chocks away!'

With his right arm now raised high, he signalled to the others. They trundled towards take-off, faster. Then, after a half turn into the wind, he was easing his throttle to the fully open position, steadily, until he could feel the response of his ailerons and rudder. The Pup could be a little bitch on take-off, for the rotary engine tended to create considerable torque. When he had tail-up Frank was holding hard right rudder. Steady ... Now he had her. There was the first thrill of real response as he eased her nose up. He was airborne.

At roughly fifty feet, Frank turned to look for the others. They were there, spread out on either side, young Cardew perhaps trailing somewhat. There would be lots of time for him to catch up.

Frank took them on up. It had been decided at briefing

that the Major would be responsible for covering their tails. No one, Frank had emphasised, would make any attack except under his instructions as Flight Commander.

On up he took them, heading south towards Bayonne and being careful to stay over his own lines as they made the climb. The Pup had quite a good rate of climb, but her advantage in a fight was best obtained at around seventeen thousand feet. At that height she could still, in the hands of a skilful pilot, out-manoeuvre anything the Germans had. This was according to the book, but Frank himself had still to face the new Albatros D.iii which was said to be twenty miles an hour faster, and to be able to dive at something like the virtical without danger of breaking up. All he could hope for that morning was that they would not meet the Boche. It would, as he knew, be better to have some idea of the men on either side of him before committing them to a fight.

Ten, twelve thousand feet. Now it was becoming really cold. Far below, Frank could see the lines of the Front, and once again he experienced that strange, God-like feeling he remembered from the year before as he looked down at the battlefield in which so many thousands of mud-encrusted men were locked in a confrontation which at times it seemed neither side could break.

Frank tested his gun for the first time—a sharp burst of twenty-five rounds. He heard, above the sound of his own engine, the others following suit. For months now the R.F.C. had been fighting an enemy which was equipped with exactly double the fire-power. Besides which, the twin Spandaus which the enemy was using had the advantage of a much superior interrupter gear. Their rate of fire was faster. Instead of the 'Pop . . . pop . . . pop . . . pop . . .' which came from his Vickers, the Boche, when he fired, produced a steady 'Rad . . . dad, dad, dad, dad'.

On up. Now the cold was becoming intense as they reached fifteen thousand and Frank turned east towards Hunland. There was a layer of high cirrus above them obscuring the sun, which must have been on their starboard bow. Frank's neck began to feel the strain of his continual search of the sky. It was six months now since he had exercised it to this extent.

He checked on the others. Young Cardew was fifty yards

to his port and a little above, as he had been instructed. The Major had allowed himself to slip behind as had been part of their plan. Delaney was fifty yards to starboard.

Again Frank tested his gun. It would be hell if he had to use it and the damned thing had frozen up at this altitude. All was well, however.

They were at seventeen thousand feet. The flight turned north; for now, Frank estimated, they had reached their twenty-mile penetration. No sign of enemy aircraft.

God, it was cold. The heavy fleece-lined flying boots were a help, but even they were of little use against this temperature.

Frank began to pray that something would happen. He found too that his mind was wandering as a result of the lack of oxygen. Constantly his thoughts flicked to memories of Sarah and the hell of that letter. It was no good. She was gone. There were moments when he would almost pretend to himself that it was all a nightmare. The letter had never arrived. He slapped his face to shake some sense into himself. He turned to the others—all apparently was well.

Weaving slightly, in order to see over the side, Frank scanned the enemy sky. It was then that he saw it—a dark shape moving slowly against cloud at perhaps no more than six thousand feet. It must be a Hun, and he looked as though he were alone.

If the cloud above them broke, allowing the sun to get through, they were in a bad position—for it was at their back. And yet the Hun was tempting.

Trap. It could be a trap.

Frank was on the point of signalling a climb to starboard, but as he was about to do so he turned to sweep his eyes over the others. As he did so, his heart almost stopped beating. Young Cardew on his port side had started into a dive towards the aircraft Frank had already seen.

The bloody fool!

Now the others were reacting. Delaney on Frank's starboard was indicating that they should follow the boy down. He seemed to be thinking that Frank had not seen Cardew or the Hun far below them.

No. There was firmness in the gesture Frank made to them. They would climb as he had indicated towards where

16

the sun must be—even if they had to go through the thick layer of cirrus above them.

In a slow climbing turn they went on up. Frank Thompson could imagine at that moment what the others were thinking. They were no doubt imagining that he was avoiding a scrap. Well, damn them. The Major had told him to lead this Flight, and that was what he was doing.

There they were. They were three thousand feet below when he saw them—five of them, and diving fast towards the lone Pup flown by Cardew. He had been right. It *had* been a trap.

Frank signalled the attack. Then he throttled back and half-rolled the Pup to pull out at the vertical. Luckily Frank had lost something like four thousand feet before they had seen the Hun which had decoyed Cardew. Now he prayed that he could get down there fast enough. Gradually he eased it out of the fierceness of the initial dive. His throttle was wide open. He was bearing down in a great sweeping arc on the Hun formation which couldn't have seen him yet. On either wing Delaney and the Major were with him.

Frank tested his guns again. The same short burst, twenty-five rounds. He was arched tensely over the control column, like a jockey.

The Pup was screaming. Down they went. Suddenly, out on his right, Frank saw the Major release a distress signal. Something was wrong with his aircraft. He was breaking off. That left two of them to cope with the five Huns, which he could now discern to be the new Albatros D.111 model.

He was going to have to meet them at an altitude which gave them the advantage.

Young Cardew, Frank could now see, was firing at the old three-strutter which was his prey. But much too soon. He was hopelessly out of range. Damn you, boy! Why couldn't you have done what you were bloody well told!

The five D.111s were closing in fast on young Cardew, who obviously had no idea of their presence. There was a terrible sinking feeling in Frank Thompson's guts, for now he knew that the Boche would get to Cardew before he could deflect them. The first of them was on to the boy now. Long streams of tracer were reaching out to him. The gunner, too, of the three-strutter was also firing at him.

Poor little bastard!

It happened quite suddenly. First there was the long stream of escaping petrol. Then the sudden flash. It was a sickening flamer: the Pup seemed to disintegrate and then fall on down like a burning oily rag.

A terrible anger seized Frank Thompson as he pressed on down. He didn't know if Delaney was still with him, and he didn't care. All he prayed for was the chance to kill, and now he had the last of the five D.111s in his sights. But the range must have been four hundred yards. Frank closed on in.

At two hundred he fired a short burst of tracer. On in. The Albatros must suddenly have become aware of Frank's presence, for suddenly he broke from his formation and went into a tight turn to starboard. Frank turned, closing fast now, and he knew the sudden fear of having a wing buckle, for he had punished the Pup dreadfully on the way down.

But he was closing. At a hundred yards, with the turning Albatros beginning to fill his sights, Frank fired a long burst. He could see the pilot twisting in his cockpit as he tried to discover exactly where Frank was. To kill the man was what Frank was aiming for. He had a horror of turning an aircraft into a flamer. So far it had never happened to him. Now all the skill he had ever developed as a boy with a gun was being used. His intention was to hit the frantic German pilot between the shoulder-blades.

But it didn't happen that way. The German aircraft seemed to stagger on to its tail and then fall over on one wing and drop. Frank had no way of knowing if he had hit the pilot or even the aircraft for that matter. It looked as though he had, but it could have been that the man was feigning destruction.

Now though there was his own tail to worry about. Vaguely a sudden rad-dad-dad-dad was around his ears. Frank, reaching around with a sudden fury in his guts, saw him coming in from about fifty yards. He kicked full left rudder, sending his Pup into a crazy flat turn, and as he did so he saw the fabric on his lower starboard plane being ripped by the thudding bullets. This was clearly no place to be.

He wrenched his stick over to port then, was on his back

18

falling with the quick plea in his mind that the fabric would hold.

Spinning, Frank fell fast, wondering all the way down where the hell Delaney might be. At two thousand feet he levelled out, searching frantically behind for any sign of the man who had been on his tail.

There was no one.

Frank cursed as he searched the sky above and behind. He tested his gun—which jammed after half a dozen rounds. Now he was really in trouble, miles behind the Hun lines with a jammed Vickers at two thousand feet. Suddenly, with a great lifting of his heart, Frank saw another Pup. It must be Delaney. He was perhaps a quarter of a mile ahead, and shooting fast towards the West.

With throttle wide open Frank pulled up the nose of the Pup until he was five hundred feet behind the one in front. Then he pushed the nose down until he was gaining twenty miles an hour on the other Pup. In minutes he had caught up. Delaney saw him, waved in greeting, and then slid under Frank until he was back in his original starboard wing position.

Five miles from the lines they had their first taste that morning of Archie. It was nothing serious. Most of the stuff was bursting above them, and with five minutes of furious weaving they were well away—or so Frank thought until he became aware of Delaney slipping down in the sky. Could he make the lines?

Frank pulled up and over the other Pup until he was in a position behind the other man to observe his progress. There was nothing Thompson could have done if they had been attacked, but at least he would be able to check on what happened to the American.

Now the lines were coming up. It was possible to see the grey-clad figures manning the trenches beneath them. They had now about twelve hundred feet in hand. Delaney should be able to make it.

Down, now at less than a thousand feet. Delaney was losing height very fast. There was no sign of any other aircraft in the sky, as far as Frank could see.

The Allied lines were coming. As far as Frank could guess Delaney now had about a couple of hundred feet in hand. His engine was apparently dead. With that rutted ground beneath them, grey as the face of a dead planet, and littered with shell-holes, Delaney would have no easy dead-stick landing.

When the American hit, he seemed to slice into a ridge of rising ground. But his tail was well down. He bounced twice, then the nose struck and the Pup had overturned. Frank went into a steep bank to port, encircling his stricken comrade.

His main fear was that the thing would burn before the American could release himself. But suddenly the ground around the upturned Pup was covered with running figures. As Frank circled, looking down at them, he saw them reach the Pup and then saw a figure stagger away from the aircraft. Delaney was free. Thompson now dropped until he was flying above them at about twenty feet.

Delaney saw him and waved a greeting, and when Thompson had acknowledged him, he turned north, staying at tree-top height as he headed along the deeply-rutted road beneath him—towards base.

It had been quite a morning.

CHAPTER TWO

Major Simpson was filled with an impotent rage as he saw the single Pup slip in over the hedge at the far end of the field and touch down to a moderately smooth landing. When the aircraft taxi-ed towards the hangars, to be greeted by the two ack-emmas who ran out to hold it, he could see that Captain Thompson was the pilot.

The C.O. marched stiffly towards Thompson as he emerged from the cockpit. Frank made no attempt to salute. He pulled the helmet from his head, and then ran a hand through his hair. He wiped the grease from his face with the sleeve of his leather flying-jacket.

'That was a rum do,' he said.

'Are they both gone?'

'No. Delaney came down behind our lines. His aircraft's broken, but he's all right. Some Archie got him on the way back across their lines.'

'But young Cardew?'

'Gone. Flamer. He was a bloody fool.'

'I thought,' the Major said, 'that his spirit was admirable.'

'Spirit be damned!' Frank held his nose between the forefinger and thumb of his right hand, and blew against them to clear his ears. 'If we had followed him down we could all have been goners——'

'Yes . . . Yes, quite . . .' The Major had been wrong on two counts and he knew it. He should not have expected Frank to lead a Flight on his first day with the Squadron; and he knew too that he, with Delaney, would have followed young Cardew down after that German observation plane. For this reason he was angry with himself.

'Let's have a drink,' he said suddenly.

In silence they walked towards the Mess, and as they approached the main entrance and Frank found himself to be gradually simmering down, he said with a renewed deference: 'You know, sir, I have the feeling that the day of the individual performer has gone. We've got to start operating as a unit in the air. This means as much training as we can pack in.'

'Yes. Yes, I agree . . .'

Frank could appreciate Simpson's difficulty. He had obviously started flying at an age which was older than most, and his experience in the air could have borne no relation to his rank. In spite of this, the old man had acquitted himself rather well that morning. Frank asked about the C.O.'s distress signal, but Simpson cut across the question as they entered the Mess.

'Indications, Thompson, are that there simply won't be time. Brigade keeps on insisting that we put up what they call the "offensive spirit" and that means putting up as many patrols as we can on the Hun side of the lines. Why a man fighting in the air cannot be offensive on our side of the lines, I don't understand.'

Frank smiled. It was the same old story. No one in the higher ranks of the Corps seemed yet to have realised that an aeroplane was not a horse.

'Cheers, Thompson.' They were both holding their drinks. 'It was too bad we had to lose young Cardew. But yours was a good show this morning. Did you wing one, by the way?'

'I could have done, sir. But unless Delaney can confirm, I can't claim. We were too far over their lines.'

The Major wrinkled his thick nose and then stroked his moustache before going on. 'What,' he said, 'made you think that three-strutter was a decoy?'

'Instinct, I suppose.' Frank coughed with embarrassment.

'Thompson'—the Major signalled for another drink, but Frank stepped closer to the bar to make it his round— 'Thompson, I can't say it here and now officially, but I see no reason why you shouldn't take over B Flight. I'll recommend to Wing Headquarters. We should have confirmation within a couple of days.'

'Thank you, sir.'

'We'll drink to that.' Major Simpson allowed himself to smile.

Frank excused himself then to make out his report with

the Adjutant. There was also the business of sending out a crew to pick up Delaney and if possible his aircraft.

It was as he was passing the mail rack in the entrance hall that he was suddenly drawn to a halt. There were some letters under 'T'. It was possible, just possible, that there might be something for him—as indeed there was. The handwriting on the envelope was Sarah's.

Instinctively Frank turned back towards the bar. Then he hesitated. Dammit, why should a woman affect him this way? An hour before he had been fighting for his life. He had just returned with an aircraft which had been ripped by a dozen bullet-holes. He had just seen a young boy go down in flames, and another fight desperately to bring a helpless Pup over his own lines and then crash. But yet this unopened letter which he now held in a hand which even trembled slightly, was frightening him more than any of that. He was afraid to open it.

Back at the bar the Major was still there. His eyebrows were raised quizzically.

'I'm sorry, sir. I thought I might have one more.'

Major Simpson saw the letter in Frank's hand. In his own way he was a man of some perception. He said quietly: 'Bad news?'

'I don't know yet, sir.' Frank took the drink he had ordered and downed it quickly in one gulp. Then he left, made out his report to the Recorder and arranged to have Delaney picked up.

It was evening, however, before he had the courage to open the letter.

The Mess was in a strange mood that night. After dinner there was a half-hearted attempt to start some kind of a thrash, but there was no real enthusiasm. The feelings of all of them were coloured by the loss of young Cardew that morning. No one mentioned his name, for that was not done, but a sense of the boy's loss was there.

Some of them, after a few drinks, started singing the Squadron song, but when they reached the one about *'There was a young pilot lay dying'* a voice from their midst shouted to them to 'Shut up!' and gradually the singing trickled to a stop.

Sitting in a corner, alone, trying to concentrate on a letter he was writing to his mother, Frank's mind kept wandering off in thought of that flaming Pup he had seen go down that morning, containing the charred, dying body of the boy Cardew. He was regretting now his impatience with the lad's impetuosity. It was a natural enough thing to have done. But—dammit all—why did they have to come into the lines without any real experience?

Frank called for another drink, and then tried to get back to the letter he was writing. It was impossible. That other letter kept coming back to him:

'Dearest Frank, I do hope my last letter was not too great a disappointment to you. I really do think that my decision is in the best interests of both of us. But it seems to me that there is no reason why we should not remain friends——'

Friends! How could they be friends? What kind of a woman was she if she imagined he could think of her as merely a friend, after what he had felt for her? Even then, sitting in the corner of the Mess with all the sound of their drinking around him, Frank could smell the loveliness of her—her neck, her eyes, the softness of her hair as he had held her against his face. There was such desire in him; not to take, but to give. To give all the life that was in him to her.

Oh, dear Sarah, how much I love you and want you, and want to be with you. I do, I do. The words were spoken within himself. His lips did not move and no sound came from him, but he could feel the words trickling through all of his body, warming him.

'Thompson, I don't believe you know Captain Babcock.'

It was the Major speaking, and he was standing against the writing-desk at which Frank was trying to compose his letter. Frank stood up to shake hands with the man Babcock.

Babcock appeared to be about three years older than Frank; dark, with a faintly grizzled look about him that suggested some kind of experience. And he wore the M.C.

'Captain Babcock has just been posted to us. He arrived this afternoon.'

Frank smiled as he took the new man's hand, but there was something about him he didn't like. Could it have been his eyes, which indicated a basic distrust?

They drank together, and in a little time were joined by some of the others. Then the Major left them to check with Wing as to what its requirements might be for the following day.

Frank, in the circle of perhaps eight or nine pilots, allowed Captain Babcock to do most of the talking. Babcock loved it. It was quickly apparent that he was intent on impressing the younger man with the extent of his experience.

There was undoubtedly something suspect about him, Frank thought. He was too anxious to buy drinks, and much too keen to talk about his own war. As far as Frank could gather, Babcock's Western Front experience had been gained in 1915, and that—as far as could be ascertained—had been achieved in artillery spotting; which was a tough job and could indeed be very hazardous. But it was a vastly different cup of tea from flying a Pup operationally in 1917.

Babcock's single-seat experience had been gathered on Home Defence in England, which was fine and would have been fine if there had not been something patronising, almost deprecatory, in the way he referred to the current scene.

But the youngsters loved it, and Frank, in a strange way, felt they were almost trying to encourage Babcock to play against him. That was it. There was a resentment in Babcock, but why Frank couldn't imagine. Perhaps it was simply the way he was made.

Next day the weather made flying impossible. All day the men hung around the Mess and their billets, waiting for the rain and low clouds to clear, but it never did. After tea the C.O. organised a lecture on Tactics. He and Frank, together with a Flight Commander—a man called Frobisher —addressed the assembled pilots. And then at the end the C.O., possibly as a courtesy, asked Babcock to speak.

It was obvious that Babcock was resentful. In a kind of snide aside he referred to Frank Thompson's evaluation of the Scout role in 1917 as being that of 'Richtoviana', his inference being that Thompson's evaluation meant that a Flight, a Squadron, perhaps even eventually a Wing, was being used for the glorification of one man's reputation. His idea was that a dogfight was a dogfight, let every man look

25

after himself, and may the best men win.

Nothing could have been further from the truth as far as Frank was concerned.

The day after the weather had cleared to some extent. It would have been possible to have the whole Squadron in the air in order to practise flying as a Squadron. Frank suggested it, for he had practised this kind of flying at Uphavon and had found that—particularly for the younger pilots—the experience was invaluable. The Major, however, vetoed the idea. They would fly in Flights. He, Major Simpson, could not envisage the day when more than four, or at the most five, aircraft at a time could be usefully deployed in aerial combat.

It was decided by the C.O. that each Flight, individually, would practise formation flying and combat tactics. It was at briefing that the Major took Frank aside. Immediately Frank sensed the other's embarrassment. For in his way Major Simpson was one of those men who invariably try to do their best by other people and inevitably end up by doing their worst.

Now the Major took Frank by the arm. 'Frank . . . er, an awkward situation has arisen . . .'

'Yes, sir?'

'Yesterday I talked to you about the possibility of your taking over B Flight——'

'That's right, sir.'

'Frank'—again the use of his Christian name—'this man Babcock, you may not realise it, but he is considerably senior to you. Now I know what I said to you a couple of days ago about taking over B Flight. Well, this morning I had a call from Wing. They think that as Babcock is your senior that he should—ah—take over the Flight Commander vacancy. In other words, that he should have B Flight. That means that on these exercises this morning I want Frobisher to have his own Flight—A; Babcock to have B, and of course C Flight's Commander, Anderson, to run his own show, as he has done since we converted to Pups . . .'

Frank said nothing for a moment and then, very quietly, and with distinct control, he said : 'Sir, I quite understand. I was more than flattered that you offered me the Flight in the first place, but in the end what matters is what you consider to be best for the Squadron.'

There was nothing the Major could say. In the end, with his somewhat conditioned crypticism, all he could reply was: 'Quite.' Then he added: 'Oh, by the way, you'll be flying in B Flight with Babcock. When Delaney gets back he'll be with you——'

It was obvious, thought Frank, that the Old Man had to some extent been influenced by the line that Babcock was so expert in shooting. Fair enough. But—God Almighty!— to move into the conditions they were now facing with a man who was still living in 1915 was, to say the least, unsettling.

At eleven that morning the three Flights took off. A led, then B, then C; in that order. Frank was flying number two to Babcock. They climbed, four of them, towards the Channel Coast. It was a fine morning and away below Frank was able to look down again on the battleground. There was always something like a feeling of guilt in him when he did this. It had been a long time since he had slogged the days away down there, yet he was never able to shake off the feeling that he should still be there with them, enduring what they were enduring.

And yet he knew that the men in the trenches were always conscious of the men who flew. Who knew?—perhaps there was some kind of an answer for all of them. It was true that the men in the trenches had to suffer the muck and the filth, but at least when all hell was breaking loose around them they could still cling to the security of Mother Earth. Up here, there was nothing at which to clutch. Not even a parachute. The powers-that-be seemed to have come to the conclusion that a parachute might weaken the resolve of an operational pilot.

Frank thought about Babcock. It was possible that he had already formed a prejudice against the man which made it impossible to see him clearly. But as they climbed—and Frank was more or less intentionally tucking himself in very close to Babcock's starboard wing—he had an uneasy feeling that the man who led the Flight was unsure of himself. There was something in the way Babcock's head darted from side to side at the men on either wing—Frank on the starboard with a youngster called Wilson on the port (there was no fourth man because of Delaney's non-appearance,

27

something about which Frank wondered)—which made him uncertain of the leader's confidence.

They did the usual things—and Frank smiled, the grease creasing on his face, as he thought of flying in England—that might have been expected from someone who had spent so long waiting for Zeppelins to come over. For an hour Babcock had them in a Vic, then in line astern, then in line abreast. To say that they practised tactics was nonsense. For how can you practise tactics unless there was some kind of target aircraft? They had none.

Babcock eventually—and one could sense his relish—signalled that they were on a let-down course for home.

It was too bad. At base there were distinct signs of a cross-wind. There was no suggestion of the leader taking them in on a formation landing; he was much too concerned about his own performance in these conditions to be worried about anyone else. He went in first.

Poor Babcock. The cross-wind got him and from where Frank was circling at five hundred feet it looked at first as though he might have held the Pup. He got a wing down, corrected and then ground-looped viciously. There appeared to be no real damage and something like a dozen erks had run towards him to help control the frisky Pup when he landed.

Young Wilson was flying alongside Thompson. Frank waved him down. There seemed to be a kind of politeness in the gesture. Wilson went on down while Frank continued to circle the field. The boy made his approach and it appeared at first that he had too much height; possibly because of the natural embarrassment of an overshoot, he put his machine into a side-slip, tricky enough at any time but in that cross-wind—for it was possible to see from the wind-sock the problem they were facing—positively hazardous.

Wilson did not recover from his side-slip in time. His aircraft hit the deck with one wing down and suddenly from his circuit height of five hundred feet Frank Thompson could see the youngster's aircraft tumbling over like a toy, then burst into flames.

Scissors cut into Frank's heart. He could see what he took to be the pilot struggling in the cockpit—for, grotesquely, the Pup had eventually landed right-side-up before exploding. It was like a nothingness. Hell.

There was no point. A Crossley tender had reached the aircraft and its complement of ground-crew were obviously trying to reach the pilot. Frank decided to go in. Down he went, treating the Sopwith Pup like a frisky young girl. Around, on to the down-wind leg, and then into his final approach. There was indeed a bitch of a cross-wind.

Frank levelled, and then dipped his starboard wings. He counter-acted the drift with one set of wings down to starboard, into the wind; then, instead of trying to get his tail down, he made a wheels-only landing, counter-acting all the time with lots of right rudder. When she settled and slowed, he allowed the tail to come down.

He carried on past the crashed aircraft, intentionally ignoring the whole situation. It was the only way to behave. At the hangars they ran out to meet him and grabbed his wing-tips, holding him in the now quickly gusting wind. He cut his switches and extricated himself from the cockpit.

'A bit of a mess, sir, over there——'

'Yes . . . yes, indeed, Corporal. What—w-what happened to Captain B-Babcock's aircraft?'

'Nothing much, sir, only undercarriage.'

That evening there was again a suggestion of the gloom that had been prevalent for the past two days. Somehow when a man—and Wilson had by no means yet been a man—is killed in his own back yard as it were—it has more effect than when he is left behind, fallen in an enemy sky into a kind of oblivion.

The C.O. that night tried to raise their spirits. All the drinks were on him. Then, when he became a little drunk, he insisted that they sang the Squadron Song. Frank was on the fringe of the company and had the distinctly unpleasant feeling of not at that moment being of it.

> 'Once there was a pilot
> So young and fancy-free
> Who climbed the mighty 'thereal
> To fight for one-five-three.
> Then there was this German
> And let us not deny
> He was the biggest bastard
> Who ever kissed the sky . . .'

It was then that the swing doors of the ante-room were pushed open and there appeared, in what was obviously tremendous form, the figure of Delaney—drunk.

They ran towards the American like a bunch of anxious Boy Scouts. Then, despite his protests, they gathered him up and carried him to the C.O., planting him at the Old Man's feet.

'Here he is, sir. Here he is. The Americans will be in the war now at any minute . . .'

'What d'ya mean? What d'ya mean? The Americans *are* in the war. I almost won it all by myself a couple days ago——'

At that they descended on Delaney. There was only one thing to do—de-bag him. And this they proceeded to carry out, with success. Not that the American cared. Lying there, looking up at them all, and wondering possibly if he would ever make his feet again, Delaney called to the C.O.:

'Glass-Arse, you're lovely. I love you, and when a Delaney says he loves you, he loves you. I'm goin' to give you a kiss.'

They helped him to his feet—for he had taken his de-bagging in good spirit—and when he was standing upright he threw his arms around the Old Man and kissed him on both cheeks.

To be fair to the Major, he took it very well. He smiled and then called out that they should bring a large drink for Delaney. In response, however, Delaney reiterated: 'Glass-Arse, I love you. What in hell happened to you the other day? Did something go wrong with the old *esprit de corps*?'

It was at that moment that Frank Thompson decided he should intervene.

'Delaney,' he said. 'Where the hell have you been for the past two days?'

'I've . . . I've been the guest of the British Royal Artillery, and if any one of you bastards doesn't agree that the British Royal Artillery is the finest outfit in the whole goddam world, then he's a goddam liar . . .'

Suddenly Delaney stopped dead in his tracks. He stared—not altogether drunkenly—at Frank for some long moments, and then he called out: 'Gentlemen——'

There was the sudden hush which is the response to a

man's conviction, even when he had been drinking as much as Delaney obviously had.

Someone said: 'Come on now, Delaney—have a drink with the C.O.'

'I will. Sure I will. Old Glass-Arse is okay. But . . .'

'But what?'

'Gentlemen, I want to introduce you to a guy who knows his business——'

'Who?' they demanded.

'Have you *got* to ask me dumb questions?' he glowered.

'Have a drink, Delaney!' None of them were taking him seriously.

'I'll have a drink when I'm good and ready. I'm goin' to tell you guys that any guy who can lead a Flight on his first offensive patrol and at the same time shoot down a Hun and—shut up, you bastards!—*and* have the guts to see me across the lines like a mother, is a goddam important pilot in my books. 'I'll drink with you, sir'—he looked across at the Major—'but I'll be drinking to Frank Thompson——'

There was a silence, then someone said: 'Do you mean to tell us that Captain Thompson had a kill on that patrol?'

'Sure he did. I saw the guy hit the deck. I'm saying it. He had a kill.'

With that, the Mess erupted. They didn't know Frank, and perhaps there were few who ever would know him, but they couldn't resist this. Delaney pushed his way through the crowd to throw his arms around Frank's neck; and Frank, embarrassed as always by any show of emotion and yet inwardly thrilled, could only try to extricate himself from their enthusiastic thumps and handshakes.

'Who are you?' Delaney had seen Captain Babcock for the first time. The Englishman was looking at him with the expression of someone who disapproved of Americans, in particular drunken Americans.

The Major introduced them.

From then on it was thrash all the way through the evening. Soda syphons were used like machine-guns. Waiters disappeared when eventually the going became really rough. At one stage Delaney rode into the ante-room on someone's motor-cycle and it was at this moment that Frank Thompson decided to retreat.

In his room a tremendous wave of sadness and regret

31

seemed to assail him. It was, of course, the drink he had taken that had brought on the depression and made him think of Sarah. Time and again, since he had received that letter at the base, his heart had sunk with the thought of her.

Normally he would know only a brief flickering of the spirit; something—a shake of the head, a word from someone else—could erase the image of her. But now it was different.

With the drink he had taken; with the built-up tension of the past few days, the deaths of those two young boys, Frank felt as though something in himself was dying. He poured another drink and cursed when he saw that he was drinking the last of the Scotch.

Sarah. Bitch. All women were bitches.

Frank unbuttoned his tunic and threw the empty glass he held against the iron stove. As he did so he heard a knock at the door of his billet.

'Come in!' he snapped.

'Sir—it's me . . .McFee!'

Frank's depression vanished on the spot. He leapt forward and grabbed hold of Sergeant McFee by the shoulders as he appeared suddenly in the doorway.

'Mac, you old bastard!'

'Sir, I'm posted. I'm posted to your Squadron. I heard you were back and . . . when I heard I had a mate of mine at Wing get me posted over here——'

'Great, Mac, great! Gosh, it's good to see you again!'

Frank's bad mood was gone now. They drank gin because there was no more Scotch left, and talked on into the night until the last of the gin had gone the way of the last of the Scotch.

It was Mac who arranged Frank on his bed. He unbuttoned his shirt and loosened his necktie. Then, smiling down at the now sleeping figure, he moved quietly towards the door and went out.

He had the feeling that he had done Frank something of a good turn by his appearance that night.

CHAPTER THREE

Next morning, Frank's batman, Maloney, had some difficulty in awakening him at six. There was a call on, but
Maloney found Frank not only deeply asleep but unconscious, virtually.

Maloney used his smelling salts and eventually Frank
became alive. Surprisingly, he felt quite well. He asked the
time and was told; he was also told that he was due to be
airborne in an hour.

'Maloney . . '

'Sir?'

'Could it be that I saw Sergeant McFee last night?'

'I believe that there is a Sergeant McFee arrived on the
Squadron, sir.'

'Maloney——'

'Would you like to change your shirt, sir?'

'To hell with my shirt!' Frank suddenly smiled at himself. He was sounding like his new American Friend. 'No
thanks—I can fly in a dirty shirt as easily as in a clean
one.'

There was a certain satisfaction in feeling as carefree as
he now felt. The tensions of the previous evening had gone.
McFee was back with him. That was something. He was
trying to remember what it was the Old Man had said on
the previous evening. But as far as Frank could remember
the Old Man had said nothing. There had been no mention
of a 'do' this morning.

The morning chilled. Frank buttoned up his collar and
straightened his tie as he tried to decide whether to go
straight to the Mess or whether to go to the Old Man's office
to discover what might be the plan. In the end he went to
the office.

Major Simpson was already there. On his deck was what was apparently a permutation of the Squadron's possibilities. Simpson did not look like a man who was at the beginning of a new day. There was a certain droop in the shoulders, a tiredness that had nothing to do with drink or lack of sleep in the man which made Frank feel for him.

'Ah, Thompson——'

'Sir?'

'There was a man, a sergeant called McFee, looking for you last night.'

'He found me, sir. He was on my last Squadron.'

'Good man?'

'Excellent, sir.'

'First-rate. They're hard to find.'

'He's a real engineer, sir. I would say the best fitter I've met in the R.F.C. Clydesdale trained.'

'Good. Frank——' Again the C.O. had dropped the formal 'Thompson' and his voice sounded concerned. 'You look dreadful. Are you feeling all right?'

'I'm fine, sir.'

'I've called briefing for half an hour from now. Let's go and have breakfast.'

Frank, strangely, did not feel at all as bad as in fact he looked. Indeed, he felt then totally in control of himself. He was even consciously aware of a feeling of unity in his body, a strange physical gathering together of all that he was.

Breakfast was a desultory affair. The thrash of the night before had left them all somewhat limp, and perhaps the prospect of an early morning offensive patrol was not the most cheering thing at that time.

Frank had a word with his armourer before making his way to the Old Man's office for briefing. He would have liked to supervise the loading of his ammo, a task they were completing now, but there was no time.

That morning's job was to be a D.O.P.—Distant Offensive Patrol—at seventeen thousand feet, twenty miles on the Hun side of lines.

When Major Simpson announced this to the assembled pilots there was something of a low rumbling from their collective body. Frank could understand this. It was not that any of the men there were lacking in what Headquarters might have called the 'offensive spirit'. It was that, intuitively, they were feeling an objection to an attitude of the High Command.

Somehow, in the minds of those who 'ran things' an aircraft was not being offensive if it were operating on its own side of the lines. This thinking no doubt came from men who had served throughout their careers as cavalry officers. An officer on a horse had indeed to look for his enemy. What Frank could not understand was how a piece of sky on one side of the lines could be more offensive than the other.

The craziness was that the British, indeed the French as well, were expected to fly slower machines deep into enemy territory and then, having possibly used up the maximum amount of fuel, have to fight their way back to base against the prevailing wind from the west.

But the offensive spirit had to be maintained and that morning it was the theme of the Major's briefing for the patrol.

Two Flights were involved—A and B. Babcock was leading B, which was comprised of Frank, Delaney and yet another green youngster, one by the name of Webster.

After the C.O.'s briefing, he had asked for questions, but there had been none. Babcock was noticeably reticent. After briefing he had a short discussion with Frank and Delaney and young Webster about Babcock's signals. But that was all. There was an uneasiness between them which Frank didn't like.

Dammit, why had this man to nurse resentment?

Encased in the tiny cockpit of the Pup, Frank suddenly saw the figure of his old fitter, Sergeant McFee, arrive on the scene. McFee waved in greeting, and as he returned it, Frank felt a sudden surge of reassurance in seeing the old bastard standing there. It was strange how some men, by the very nature of their being, could radiate a confidence. It was a kind of animal quality.

Frank switched on and pumped fuel into his carburettor. The man at his prop stood back, waiting for a signal.

'Contact!'

'Contact!'

The morning chill made starting difficult. Four times, five, that prop was swung with attendant curses. Then, as

35

he flicked the throttle and caught it, the engine roared into life. The rigger leapt back and there was much laughing and signals of triumph to the cockpit.

Now Frank could see that the others, with the exception of the new boy, Webster, had their engines running. The whole airfield seemed to be leaping into life. Webster's engine was turning now. Frank could see Delaney arranging his helmet and goggles, trying to settle himself comfortably into the cockpit. There was a need for each of them to arrange themselves as comfortably as possible. It was as though, by doing so, you became more effectively at one with the aeroplane.

Babcock raised his right arm as a signal to move, and the four aircraft of B Flight rolled forward and turned towards take-off point.

The morning air was smooth so that they climbed easily, loosely, line abreast, towards the seventeen thousand feet which was their objective. Far below—for it was possible in this loose formation to relax momentarily—Frank could see the lines between Ypres and Dickebusch. Men were trapped there under the constant hail of German artillery, poor devils.

It was possible too, to visualise the great movement of men and materials which was taking place behind the lines. It was obvious that yet another tremendous push must be on the way, and it occurred to Frank as he nursed his Pup on its way up alongside the others that some kind of action was in preparation. Perhaps the pilots were being kept in the air in an attempt to draw the Hun away from the Allied lines so that they would see nothing of the preparations taking place.

Every so often Babcock turned the formation to the east in order to fire off a few rounds. A Flight were on their port side and a little above them. Now they were swinging in a wide arc across into Hunland. It was strange to think that down there was the committed enemy, grovelling in his trenches as the Allies were, probably cursing the war just as the Tommies did, endlessly. The whole world seemed to have moved in a direction from which it could not turn.

On their starboard there suddenly appeared a formation of four Triplanes. They were probably Naval planes. But they were climbing faster than the Pup could. Why was it that the bloody Senior Service had to have the best of everything?

They were around sixteen thousand feet when all hell broke loose.

No one appeared to have seen anything of the Huns until they struck. Certainly Frank had seen no signal from Babcock. When the first of the Hun tracer hit, a great searing shock seemed to go through him. He looked up and there— coming straight down at them out of the early morning eastern sky—was a complete formation of Huns, all brightly coloured and flashing fire.

B Flight broke and as the leading Germans went straight on through them and into A Flight, so did the others. The sky had become a crazy pattern of whirling aircraft. Vertically, and turning as tightly as he dared pull the Pup, Frank fired a short burst as he saw a gaudily painted green and yellow Hun move into his line of sight. Nothing happened.

Now the smell of cordite filled his nostrils. There was someone on his tail and firing fast. Wrenching his neck around he could see the man on his tail. He was so close, perhaps thirty yards, that Frank imagined he could glimpse him smiling.

Rip-tracer went searing past. There was only one thing to do. Frank kicked his machine into a flat, ungainly turn. It was clumsy flying but it was survival flying. His enemy swept on past and as the man did so, Frank felt himself breathing hard through his mouth. It was as though he were making a kind of desperate, clutching gesture at life.

Terror struck as the Pup came straight at him—one of his own, or perhaps one of A Flight. They couldn't have been more than thirty to forty yards apart. This idiot had come out of a turn, right into Frank's line of flight.

There was no time to do anything. Would the other go down? Would he go up? Which way would he turn?

Instinctively—there was no time for any intelligent reaction—Frank cut his throttle and kicked full right rudder and stick. It felt as though he were disembowelling the Pup ... But, oh God, they had struck!

Panic—there was no other word for it—seized Frank. There was no way of telling what damage he had sustained.

37

At first there was no way of knowing if he were still flying. There had only been the sickening, jarring crunch. The Pup seemed to shudder and then tilt as though about to fall over some endless precipice. Was there pressure on the stick?

There was.

Crazily, he had hit someone, and it felt as though his own aircraft were still flying. With his throttle almost closed he pushed the nose down until he could sense a reaction on his ailerons.

But where was the other man?

There was a sickness now in Frank's guts as he turned his head frantically in search of the man with whom he had been in collision.

At first there was nothing. Even the whirling Huns who had attacked them seemed to have gone. There was nothing above. God, where was the man he had hit? Was he still flying?

The engine, after an initial roughness, seemed to be running smoothly. From side to side, Frank weaved on down using his control column and waiting with each movement for its failure to respond. But no, he was still flying.

Then he saw the other Pup. It was perhaps four or five thousand feet beneath him, and it was falling like a leaf from a tall tree on a quiet autumn afternoon. Poor devil. Frank could see now that the starboard upper mainplane had crumpled back. It was just possible too to see the figure of the man in the cockpit; he seemed to be half-standing as though trying to decide whether or not to jump.

It was a helluva choice, but whoever it was making it decided to stay with the aircraft. Frank followed on down, slowly circling; transfixed, he watched the man he had struck falling to his doom.

As he turned towards the west Frank Thompson was heedless of the possibility of being attacked. In a way he didn't care. At that moment he was a sitting duck for any Hun who cared to take a casual swipe at him. Something had happened, something nightmarish; something he had prayed would never happen.

There was a sick fascination in watching the Pup go on down. It hit some fairly thick woodland, and as it did so it seemed to disintegrate.

Involuntarily Frank's stomach was heaving. His eyes had misted now until he could see nothing. He tore at his goggles and as he did so he uttered a kind of animal howl of rage.

Whom had he struck? Was it Delaney? Was it Babcock? Was it the new boy, Webster? Jesus, God, it didn't matter —one of his own people had gone down uselessly.

Not until he levelled off—for it gradually dawned on him that if he were to survive he shouldn't lose too much height until he had established the nature of the damage to his own machine—did Frank realise that all was far from well.

With its nose down there didn't appear to be too much wrong with the Pup, but flying straight and level there was a marked tendency to fly right wing down. His eyes ran frantically over his own mainplanes but there was nothing he could see to be wrong.

He tried to work out how he must have hit the other man. Of course! It was his undercarriage. When he had pulled up and over to starboard, his undercarriage must have hit the other man's starboard upper plane. That was why he hadn't seen him when they had struck.

Now he had a battle on his hands.

The sun was well up, but dangerously behind him. Common sense was beginning to return; he was regaining control of his reactions. He began to swing the Pup violently from side to side in the vague hope that if his undercarriage were hanging loose, the damned thing would fall off. But it was a vain hope.

Then the first of the Ack-Ack burst too close for comfort on his starboard bow. This was no place to be! Such had been his concern with the collision and then with the problem of working out exactly what was wrong with the Pup, that he had given practically no thought as to where he might be. He was heading west, towards his lines; that was all he knew.

As the ugly black balls burst around him, it was practically impossible to weave. The damned Pup wasn't controllable enough for that. But he had to do something. He looked at his altimeter: nine thousand. He had nine thousand feet in hand and unless he wanted to be ripped to pieces by the shrapnel which the Hun gunners were sending up at him, he would have to sacrifice some of this precious height in order to confuse them.

To starboard she slipped easily down. So he cut his throttle right back. It was all he could do. In one long searing side-slip to starboard he dropped like the proverbial stone until he had lost another three thousand feet. The Archie was bursting above him. He opened full throttle and now, because he felt that with its nose down, the Pup was behaving more responsively, he decided to lose a couple of hundred feet a minute.

Where was he?

Now the lines were beneath him and now that he was again in control of his faculties, he was conscious of the danger which surrounded him. He didn't even know if his guns were working properly. But he daren't fire in the direction in which he was flying. He could have done, of course, but there was something in Frank which wouldn't allow him to fire towards his own lines. Already that day he had had one disaster. It was unthinkable that even a stray, spent bullet should hit someone on his own side of the lines.

The damned Pup was now being really difficult. A constant drag was pulling him to starboard and as he slid on down towards Ypres itself—which he could now see rising out of the early morning mist—Frank began to think of the problem facing him when he attempted a landing.

Obviously any kind of attempt at a normal touchdown might lead to disaster. First, he'd find the field and then he'd have to play it by ear.

Base came out of the early morning mist like a jewel being offered on a rich, green velvet cushion. Frank knew he was about to crash; it was only a question of how.

At five hundred feet he could see, as he raised his goggles and looked down, that they were aware of his difficulty, but to make sure he opened and closed his throttle in quick succession. Most of the others of A and B Flights were now back, and it was only then that Frank realised how slowly he must have been travelling.

To make a circuit was impossible. He decided to go straight in from the approach; there was only a slight breeze, nothing that could cause any real trouble. He cut back his throttle and immediately had to counteract the immense drag by throwing his stick over hard to port.

The approach was much too fast, but it had to be. At a hundred feet he switched off in order to reduce the hazard of fire when he finally hit. It was now a dead-stick landing.

At ten feet he levelled off. The tail was very far down, for it was his intention to drop in from that height; any attempt at a normal touch-down would have meant that the starboard wing might have trailed and resulted in a cartwheel.

It was hell holding up his starboard mainplanes, but gradually at that angle of incidence his speed fell off and she stalled. He hit the grass like a lumpen pancake.

Frank could not in retrospect have pieced together what happened then. She did not burn, though, and the first he saw of the Pup was when he had run perhaps fifty yards from the crumpled wreck—literally into the arms of Sergeant Hamish McFee.

CHAPTER FOUR

'Sir . . . Sir . . . Are you all right?'

Frank didn't know. He halted, breathing heavily. Then he felt himself, ribs and limbs, as though looking for something. He was in one piece. He removed his goggles.

'Fine, Mac. I'm all right.'

'It doesn't look as though we'll put that one together, sir.'

'No . . . No, it doesn't.'

'What happened, sir?'

'Collision, Mac——'

'Christ!'

Now Frank could see some of the others, led by Major Simpson, hurrying towards him. With the Sergeant trailing slightly behind him Frank walked in their direction. At the approach of the C.O., Sergeant McFee, no doubt conceding valour to discretion, turned back towards the wrecked Pup.

'Sir . . .'

From half a dozen yards away, Major Simpson called out : 'Good to see you, Frank. Thank God you made it!'

Frank stood quite still. Nervously he fingered the wispy moustache he wore, and then tried to speak. But the old stammer caught in his throat and for some moments the words would not come.

'Frank, let's have a drink. You deserve one for bringing that thing down—even if it's not in one piece.' The C.O. attempted a smile.

'No, no,' said Frank. Then : 'W-who was it?'

Almost brusquely, Major Simpson said : 'It was Babcock.'

Oh god!

In the Mess Frank said to Major Simpson and Delaney,

who had joined them: 'Let's get out of here.' He had suddenly become aware of something like hostility. Perhaps he had imagined it, but he felt it keenly in the attitude of those others in the room.

'No.' It was Delaney who spoke, roughly now. 'Have another drink. For Christ's sake, don't be like this, Frank. What happened could have happened to anyone. Jesus, the miracle is that you didn't both spin in. How the hell you got that thing home with the wheels hanging off, I'll never know! Probably no one else in the Squadron could have done it. Eh, Major?'

The Major nodded assent.

'Th-that's not the p-point,' said Frank, and there was a tense anger in his words. 'How d'you think I feel—knocking that poor devil down like that? He could hardly fly a Pup, far less fight one. You know that.'

'Frank, please . . .' Major Simpson spoke quietly. 'Babcock wasn't a boy. He was an experienced pilot.'

'He was an experienced pilot in 1915. He knew as much about conditions today as my Aunt Fanny!'

Behind Frank's anger was the thought that Babcock had arrived after he himself had been given B Flight. The Old Man had had to give the Flight to Babcock. Frank had accepted that, but that this should have happened; that he should be the one instrumental in destroying the man who had stood in his way. It was damnable.

Delaney smiled a smile he didn't feel. Then he said slowly: 'You're not being very sensible about this, Frank——'

The Major spoke slowly, almost with diffidence. 'Let's go to my office and make out the report with Adj. You'd better come too, Delaney.'

The Adjutant—in the R.F.C. he was generally referred to as the Recorder, although men like Frank who had been with Infantry usually thought of him as the Adjutant—was named Captain Gemmell, an old soldier in his fifties. A decent enough type, Frank had concluded. As they entered the office the Adjutant was on the telephone.

He looked up with something of a startled expression on his face. 'Frank,' he said, one hand over the telephone's mouthpiece, 'this call is for you. A woman——'

'I don't want to speak to any woman. T-tell her to go to h-

43

hell or p-phone back or something.'

The Adjutant apologised to the caller and hung up. The report on what had happened that morning was prepared. Mostly Delaney's words were used.

That afternoon another Operation Patrol was planned, to take off just after lunch. Delaney would lead B Flight. Frank had just returned from his billet after cleaning up when he saw the listings. There was only one thing to do. He went straight to the C.O.'s office.

The Old Man wore his customary worried expression. He acknowledged Frank's salute with a casual nod.

'Sir?'

'Yes, Frank.'

'I see that I'm not listed for this afternoon's O.P.'

'That's right; you have no aircraft.'

'Sir, I realise that. But you've listed young Webster. I could take his——'

'Look, Frank, I realise how you feel. I really do. But you've had a rough morning. I suggest you take it easy today and go back tomorrow to the pool at St. Omer and pick up a new aircraft. Adj. has already arranged that they have one for you.'

'I can still go tomorrow, sir. But I want to be on this afternoon's do. I r-really d-do, sir.'

Simpson looked at the floor, then he turned to take his stick, which was leaning against a filing cabinet. His eyes went to Frank's face.

'Frank,' he said slowly. 'It's my job to decide these things.'

'I realise that, sir.' Frank stiffened.

'Let me put you in the picture.' Major Simpson turned towards a map hanging on the wall and pointed: 'South of here, right now there's the most almighty battle taking place around Arras. That's where most of the Corps effort is taking place——and, I might add, where most of the Corps' losses are taking place, too. Richthofen's down there . . .'

'But——'

'Let me go on. Any minute now, as you can see from the activity behind our Front, there's going to be a big push, to help relieve the effort at Arras. Just as Arras is helping, we hope, the French effort on the Aisne . . .'

44

'Sir, I still think——'

'Let me get on!'

'Sorry.'

'Any day now we're liable to be moved south to the Arras front if things get too hot down there. Any day now. I want my best men—men who are capable of leading in the air—to be available for that eventuality.'

'I agree, sir.'

'Then?'

'Just . . .' Frank raised his right hand and clenched his fist. 'Just let me get this morning out of my system.'

It seemed a long time before the C.O. answered. His voice, when he spoke, had a warm ring to it.

'All right,' he said. 'You can take Webster's place. Delaney will still lead the Flight.'

Frank was just finishing lunch when the orderly came to his table and said that there was a telephone call for him. Who the hell? thought Frank. As though reading his thoughts, the orderly said that the caller was a lady.

A lady?

Frank could only think of the dental appointment he had tried to arrange. A tooth had been giving him a little trouble, especially when flying at high altitudes, and he had been hoping to have something done to it. But right now dentistry was the last thing on his mind.

'She seemed rather insistent, sir.'

'Tell her to go to the devil, Corporal. It's probably the base hospital at St. Marie-Cappel trying to fix a dental appointment.'

Delaney was sitting next to Frank and he said: 'You're crazy, man. If a woman was calling me right now I'd answer her even if she looked like the back-end of a horse.'

The table roared with laughter, and Frank cut across it as he said to the Corporal: 'Tell her I'm not available. But get a number I can call back. I'll ring her later.'

'Tell her *I'll* ring her, Corporal.' It was Delaney who spoke. 'I'm much more fun—guaranteed!'

The afternoon's patrol was uneventful. It was still possible to see the endless movement of troops behind the front over which they climbed. It was a lazy afternoon. Away to the north-west, as Delaney led them up behind their own lines, it was possible to see in the clarity of that April light, Dunkirk and then the glistening Channel.

Inevitably, with the vision of those white cliffs in his mind's eye, Frank's thoughts swung towards Sarah. Darling Sarah! Even the deep oily smell of the Pup he was flying, and the rich hum of the Rhone in front; even the chill at ten thousand feet and the stiff pressure of slipstream against his face, could not dispel the presence of the girl, evoked by that brief vision of far-off England.

They saw nothing that afternoon. Once, far below, Frank glimpsed what he took to be a Hun two-seater. He signalled to Delaney, who indicated that he would go down if they would give him cover from above. Frank and the two others who were with him did so, but before Delaney could get near the two-seater he had been spotted and the Hun had slipped away.

It was tea-time when they arrived back. Frank felt better. On the return trip Delaney had broken the formation when he had become bored by the inaction of the patrol; so it had been possible to be alone again in the sky. They had headed east over the Houthulst Forest, and then over the lines five miles north of Ypres. From there, Frank had headed west on his own, towards Poperinghe, north of the place, low until he picked up the road from Cassel heading back east towards the front, flying all the time now at fifty feet and less.

There had been a glorious sense of well-being and power in skipping along that road at a hundred and ten miles an hour, waving as he went to the endless stream of moving Tommies, their horses slowly dragging artillery towards the positions they would be taking up for the push that must be coming soon.

Suddenly it had occurred to Frank that there might be danger in flying over that road as he was doing. One of the Tommies could have mistaken him for a Hun, and it didn't take more than one bullet in the right—or wrong—place to bring down a Pup. He swung away from the road and flew on over the war-torn fields, punctuated here and there by the sight of some French peasant still patiently cultivating the earth of his fathers as though the greatest war in history were not taking place all around him.

This Pup of Webster's handled beautifully. Frank picked

up Dickebusch Lake, flew across it very low until he saw his airfield, then after a very low circuit of the field, he pulled up to five hundred feet. He cut the engine and side-slipped into an easy three-point landing.

When he had taxi-ed up to Dispersal and climbed out, Sergeant McFee was there. The Sergeant was beaming all over his homely face.

'That was better, sir. That was more like it!'

Frank climbed down and laughed. 'You're right, Mac,' he said. 'We can't afford many more like this morning.'

A patrol of two aircraft was ordered for six-thirty that evening, and Frank would have volunteered for that too if he had thought that the Old Man would have worn the suggestion. He didn't dare, however. Instead, with Delaney and one or two others, he went by tender to the little cemetery in the village three miles away where young Wilson had been buried.

The Squadron carpenter had constructed a cross from a propellor which was erected over the grave. The padre said a few words, and some shots were fired in salute. Frank couldn't help wondering what meaning there was in the gesture.

With Delaney he decided to walk back to the Mess instead of taking the tender which had brought them. There was something in Delaney's personality which was relax-ing. Being with the easy-going American was a kind of balm to the tremor of that day.

They had walked quite a way and were almost in the village when Delaney first spoke. He said: 'It doesn't seem right . . .'

'What doesn't?'

'Us putting up wooden crosses to that kid on a day like this.'

'Does it matter what kind of day it is?'

'Yeah, in a way it does. It matters because—Gee, I don't know, but somehow I don't remember being as conscious of spring—other springs—as I've been of this one. That kid was kind of in the spring of his life, as you might say . . .'

'In the trenches you'd have thrown an old sack over him and forgotten about him,' Frank said. 'That's what they're doing down at Arras now . . .'

'I suppose so.' Delaney spoke as though he were speaking

47

to himself. 'That's the difference with us——'

'In what way?'

'This job. It gives you a kind of identity.'

As they walked on through the edges of the strangely peaceful village—for by some miracle or accident it was wearing surprisingly few scars of war—Frank was thinking of Babcock's face. He could see it very clearly in his imagination, the slightly querulous distrust in his expression, which could have been a distrust of himself, a kind of secret fear.

Maybe in some misty other world that face was snarling its hatred of the man whose wheels had torn the wings from his aircraft and sent him plunging to his death. Frank breathed deeply, as though trying to draw into his own consciousness all the warm smells of that spring afternoon.

'*Bon jour, padre*...' Delaney bowed rather more fulsomely than was necessary to the local priest, who was scurrying past them on his rounds.

'He doesn't like us,' Frank suggested.

'You're not kidding. None of them do. Would you, if a bunch of Frenchmen built an airfield right next to your back yard in Merry England?'

'I suppose not.'

'Hey—let's take in the town!' Delaney had seen the local estaminet, for now they were walking down the straggling main street of the village.

'No, let's go back.' Frank didn't like the look of the place. From outside all that could be seen was a cavernous entrance. Some tables were grouped outside, where one old man sat with a filthy-looking dog at his feet.

'Come on. Madame's a great beauty and her sister even more so. One snag is that they hate the English. You can pretend you're German. Maybe they don't mind them.'

'No...' Still Frank hesitated.

'Oh, come on! Let's get where the action is.'

Frank yielded and they stamped into the Bar Richelieu.

'See!' Delaney cried, as they realised the place had a name. 'Richelieu slept here. Ain't that something to write home about?'

Madame appeared and Delaney ordered absinthe.

'No, no!' Frank protested.

'Cognac. You gotta drink cognac.'

'Some wine . . .'

'You can't drink the wine here, man. Be quiet. It's cognac.'

And so, after they had taken a quick reconnoitre of the bar's interior, they settled outside with a bottle of cognac. Once or twice a local peasant slipped into the place and then out again. The customers were mostly old, or very young spindly children on some errand for their elders. No one showed any sign of friendliness towards the two airmen sitting there.

'This is the life . . .' Delaney unbuttoned the R.F.C. tunic he wore. 'Yeah, man . . . If the folks at home could only see me now, sitting here at the wicked centre of this damned great metropolis, drinking real French brandy. Gee!'

Frank drank steadily, smiling occasionally at his friend but making no real contribution to the conversation. It was enough to feel the warmth of the brandy reaching down into him, and to be basking in the peace of that sleepy street. Only occasionally could they hear the low distant rumble of the early evening guns.

'What's the matter?' asked Delaney suddenly.

'Nothing.'

'You can't fool me. Something's up.'

'I was thinking about that dreary trip tomorrow in a tender all the way to St. Omer——'

'Do you a world of good. Great for the liver.' Delaney reached across with the bottle and refilled Frank's glass.

'Casey——'

'Hold it! You're getting affectionate——'

'No, really . . .' Frank's voice tailed off.

Delaney gave him a sympathetic glance. 'What's the matter? Is it Babcock?'

'Yes, in a way. I feel for the poor bastard.'

'Well then, let's drink to him.'

They raised their glasses and, in unison, said slowly as they went through the motions of the toast: ' "Never above you, never below you, always at your side." '

'Okay, That's Babcock taken care of,' said Delaney. 'Now let's forget the guy. What's the real trouble?'

'Real trouble?'

'Yeah. Who's the woman?'

'Woman?'

49

'Stop repeating like a damn parrot. You know what I'm talking about—a woman.' Delaney went through a kind of pantomime description of a voluptuous female figure. 'Like Madame Bertier here who runs the bar. She's a woman. Madame Bertier——' He raised his voice.

Madame came scurrying from the interior of the bar.

'Monsieur?'

'Madame Bertier,' Delaney asked, 'Will you marry me?'

'Monsieur!' The woman—she was tall and somewhat astringent in her general appearance, gothic almost—covered her face with her hands, thereby revealing the fact that she understood more English than she admitted to.

'Madame Bertier, I have asked you a very serious question.'

'Please, Monsieur!'

In an aside, Delaney turned to Frank, who was smiling broadly now. 'She would, you know, if only to get an American passport. In fact, if it were possible she'd probably try to get her sister into the act as well. I know these women——'

'Casey, what do you want?' Frank was embarrassed now for the Frenchwoman.

'I want'—and as he spoke Delaney stood up and bowed gracefully—'I want, Madame, a bottle of champagne . . .'

'Champagne, Monsieur? It is impossible!'

'Madame, not only is it impossible. It is extremely necessary.'

'Necessary?'

'Sit down, Casey!' Frank ordered. 'We don't need champagne.'

'Be quiet. If we're going to talk about a woman, of course we do!' Delaney turned to Madame Bertier again; his voice was heavy with seriousness. 'This gentleman and myself are discussing matters that are of the utmost seriousness to the conduct of the war.'

At this the woman appeared to be somewhat dazed.

'La guerre,' she said slowly.

'Si . . . Oui . . . La guerre . . . La victoire.'

'But, Monsieur——'

'One bottle, Madame, only one.'

She didn't smile. There was nothing on her face which could have been described as an expression. But she disappeared into the dim recesses of the bar.

'See, I told you,' Delaney said. 'She'll bring champagne.'

'You're mad!'

'When it comes you can tell me how mad you are. Brandy's a man's drink. For women we have to drink champagne cocktails. I'll mix them—even if the champagne's warm.'

'Casey, I'd rather not talk about it.'

'Look——' Delaney was still searching for the words he wanted to use when Madame returned with a bottle of what appeared to be rather old and good champagne. He leapt to his feet. 'Madame, I love you! And even if you won't marry me, I'll marry you. Promise!'

With the bottle of champagne open, Delaney mixed it with the brandy they already had. Then, when he had tasted the mixture and sighed with appreciation, he said: 'Okay, shoot. Tell all to Uncle Casey.'

Frank was silent, sipping his drink.

'Go on,' urged Delaney.

'You wouldn't understand . . .'

'Frank . . .' Delaney spoke slowly. 'Be sure about one thing. I've had more women than you've had hot dinners——'

Still Frank said nothing, and as he sat there, jaws tightly clenched, holding his glass firmly, Delaney realised that perhaps he was on the wrong tack. He allowed his friend to be silent for a while, then he said:

'Talking about it sometimes helps, y'know.'

So Frank talked then, as perhaps he had never done before. Talking about oneself was not something done in Frank's world. But he did then. He told of meeting Sarah and of how he had come to love her. He told of his family's reservations because of his financial position, and then he told of her father's attitude.

'How did she feel about all this—the money and the inheritance business?' Casey asked once.

'She was . . . she was determined to fight it out with me,' Frank said.

'So what went wrong?'

'I don't know. Someone . . . I suppose she must have been influenced by her father. I don't know.' Frank went on to tell the other man about arriving back at the pilot's pool in

France to find the letter Sarah had sent him. But he spoke as though trying to defend her, as though the letter had been written on her behalf, and not by Sarah herself.

Delaney sensed this, but for some moments he said nothing. He allowed Frank to go on.

Frank had been silent for a while before Delaney spoke. When he did, he said: 'It must have been kind of rough, getting that letter.'

'Yes.'

'There are guys who could have cracked up, getting a letter like that.'

Frank nodded, almost absently.

'Especially guys in your position—or mine. Guys who're waiting to go up front, climb into an aeroplane and get themselves shot at.'

'What d'you mean?' Frank looked up as though Delaney's words had jerked him from some private line of thought.

'I mean,' Delaney said steadily, 'She might have thought of that before writing that letter.'

Frank bristled. 'She couldn't know,' he said. 'She couldn't even guess what it's like out here.'

'There are a helluva lot of newspapers trying to tell her.'

Frank glowered. 'I knew you wouldn't understand.'

'Okay, okay, so I don't understand . . . Let's have a drink. After wasting all that charm on Madame B, I'm not going to waste the goddam stuff.'

Huge beakers of brandy and champagne were now poured out, and Delaney allowed Frank to drink his before he went on to say: 'I understand one thing——'

'What's that?'

'A guy is wasting his time if he tries to give another guy any kind of advice about love.'

'Casey, I'm sorry. I just didn't want to talk about it.'

Delaney emptied his glass and then filled it again. He placed a hand on Frank's shoulder.

'Frank,' he said, 'If I tell you that I know your feelings, I don't expect you to believe me. But understand this——'

Frank looked uncomfortable. 'I know you're only trying to help, but I'd much rather you didn't——'

'Sure you do. Well, let me tell you—I've been hurt by women, too. I've never known a man worth his salt who hasn't. It's not that women deliberately set out to hurt a guy, any more than guys set out to hurt women. It's the situation——'

'What do you mean?'

'It's the situation, and it's the time. How do I put it?'

Frank shook his head a little muzzily. The drink was beginning to have an effect on him.

'I don't follow you . . .'

'Let me try to tell you. It's like . . . it's like not only with men and women, it's like any human situation. You've got to be mutual.'

'Mutual?'

'Yeah. Before I got into this job I did a lot of things—one of them was a spell in vaudeville. Not performing—I left that to the idiots. No, I was in what you might call management for a while. I saw a lot of people, Frank, a lot of talent—performers and managers. But I never saw any one of them get anywhere unless they had the luck to get together in the right place at the right time. Unless their need, their hunger, was what I call mutual——'

'What's this got to do with Sarah and me?'

'Well, from what you've told me, she's one helluva nice girl—and I don't need to tell you what I think of you. But it seems to me, Frank, that the trouble is that your needs right now aren't mutual.'

'We love each other——'

'Really nice people will always find a dozen or so folk in their lives whom they could love. That's what makes it all so complicated as time goes on.'

'I could never love anyone like I love Sarah.' Frank helped himself to another drink, downing it greedily. He was by this time not only somewhat muddle-headed but slightly maudlin.

'Sure, not in exactly the same way,' said Delaney, 'But what really makes it work, in my experience, is when you meet someone whose time and place is your time and place. When that happens, it works. That's why it so seldom works. It never has for me—yet.'

Frank smiled without feeling anything remotely approaching mirth. 'Do you think we could have another bottle of champagne?' he asked.

'Yeah, sure. Why the hell not?'

So they did, and they drank until even the natives looked friendly. They started their walk back towards the Mess and dinner, then caught up with a man driving an ox-cart who agreed to take them the rest of the way for a few francs. They slept until he woke them at the airfield.

Dinner was almost over, but a friendly orderly promised to try to 'rustle up something'. It was as they were seated for the meal that another orderly came towards Frank. There was a second telephone call for him.

Frank couldn't believe it. Those people must really be anxious about his teeth! Was it the same woman who had called before? What was her name?

The man hadn't been able to catch it. But it had come from the hospital at St. Marie-Cappel. A Sister-someone.

That, Delaney decided, was what Frank needed in the circumstances—a sister.

'Heh!' Suddenly the American had a great idea. To-morrow, he said, Frank would be within ten miles of St. Marie-Cappel when he went to St. Omer to pick up his new Pup. Why didn't he call at the hospital and get acquainted with this new-found sister?

It was a great idea. Frank said he would do that.

The food they ate was cold and had little effect on the brandy and champagne they had consumed. So, after they had eaten, there was only one thing left to do—have some more brandy and champagne.

They did.

CHAPTER FIVE

The tender for St. Omer had been waiting for half an hour before Frank was ready to go. The only blessing in an otherwise totally bleak prospect was that he didn't have to fly, even to St. Omer. He couldn't have found the far edge of the field.

' 'Morning, Corporal.'

' 'Morning, sir. We'll have to move a little fast, I'm afraid. We're late. I hope you don't mind, sir . . .'

'I don't mind, Corporal. Anything you say.' God, what had that Delaney done to him on the previous evening? And what was Delaney himself feeling like now? He must by this time be flying at something like sixteen thousand feet. Frank decided that he would never drink again.

'Corporal . . .'

'Yes, sir?'

Frank's spine was trying to push off the top of his head as the hard-tyred tender rattled its way along the rutted country road which, unfortunately, was still free of other traffic, thereby making it possible for the driver to travel at a speed that rendered Frank distinctly uncomfortable.

Once they hit the Ypres–Poperinghe road, however, things improved. Great masses of transport were making their way towards the Front. Frank had never seen anything like it. He said so to the driver at his side, but the man limited his comment to a laconic: 'Take it from me, sir, there's something big coming off.'

Indeed there must have been. It took them almost an hour to travel the three miles into Poperinghe, and then another three hours before they reached St. Omer, via Cassel. Frank was exhausted by the time they approached the entrance of No. 1 Aircraft Depot.

The Depot was the pool supplying the Northern Front with replacement pilots and aircraft. It was a great sprawling mess of a place, littered with Bessoneau canvas hangars, workshops and the Nissen huts that provided living quarters. It was from here that Frank had been posted to his new Squadron on his return to France, and it was here that he had received that letter from Sarah which had reduced his life to ashes.

By now it was lunch-time. The equipment officer he had been instructed to contact had gone to his Mess for lunch and it was there—after much trouble—that Frank finally located him.

When Frank found his man—a busy-moustached Captain of somewhat elderly appearance—it seemed there might be some difficulty in getting off that afternoon. Meanwhile, if Frank had a drink and something to eat, and stayed in the Mess, he would be contacted.

The place was full of men just out from England, most of them for the first time—pink-faced youths, some with wispy moustaches, worn no doubt in an attempt to give their fresh young faces an air of authority.

At lunch Frank was assailed with questions as to how things were at the Front. The place seethed with rumours. Had he heard that the average life of a pilot on the Arras Front was three weeks? Did he know that Von Richthofen had shot down his thirty-fourth victim?

Frank was struck by the lack of concern with which these boys talked of such things. They themselves were waiting for postings to Squadrons. The statistics they referred to could have applied to themselves, yet with that infinite capacity that human beings have for believing that it will always be the other fellow, they cheerfully retailed these rumours as though they applied to another species.

Possibly, though, these men were luckier than those who had been sent to No. 2 Aircraft Depot at Candas, near Doullons. It was from there that the Southern Front was being supplied. The place had a reputation even worse than that of St. Omer, and it was from Candas that the turnover in human life was truly appalling.

Frank hung around the rather dismal ante-room of the be-Nissened Mess waiting for the call which would tell whether or not he would be able to get back to his own base that day. He prayed that he would not have to spend the night here. What the hell would he do in this dump?

At four the call came from his equipment officer friend. No, he was sorry, but the aircraft he had to take back would not be ready until the following morning. Sorry again, but that was the best they could do.

Well, damn it!

Most of the youngsters who had been hanging around the place had gone back to their billets, presumably to clean up in preparation for whatever revelry they could contrive for the evening. Frank decided that he had better find himself a bed for the night.

He had done that, and had inspected the place when he remembered the telephone calls of the previous day. Delaney had been right; the hospital at St. Marie-Cappel could only have been ten miles away. If he could find some form of transport he could go across there, and perhaps have the tooth attended to—at least have the opportunity of seeing the girl who had been so anxious to contact him the previous day.

It was the equipment officer whom he had spoken to at lunch time, and who had given him the news about his Pup who provided the solution. There was a motor-cycle Frank could have, provided he took damn good care not to break the thing, and provided he told no one where he had borrowed it.

Astride the machine, Frank felt like seventeen again. Out of the main gate he found the road to Cassel—St. Marie-Cappel was somewhere to the south of the little town. He would find it.

Conditions were not as bad as they had been that morning, and in fact Frank made fairly good time until he had reached the approaches to Cassel. Then no one seemed to know the best road for St. Marie and for half an hour he was lost. Eventually he was able, in his halting French, to ask a man leading a dog cart as to his best direction, and the man—incredibly—seemed to understand him.

In twenty minutes he was outside the gates of the hospital. There was some kind of a guard there, but nothing serious. No one questioned him.

57

The main reception hall of the hospital had all the antiseptic neutrality that such places possess. He hated it on sight; the sad faces of the men being wheeled towards corridors that must have had no ending, the brisk efficiency of nurses and orderlies whose feeling for the pain they were witnessing must be in doubt.

'Can I help you, sir?' A pleasant-faced girl asked the question.

Frank explained. Someone—a Sister he imagined, whose name he stupidly did not know—had been trying to contact him throughout the previous day. He thought it might be about a dental appointment.

The girl went off and Frank waited, sinking into a sad reverie at the thought of all those broken lives this place contained. He had waited for perhaps twenty minutes when he saw Sarah.

She approached at first slowly, then as he stood up, his face registering something of the disbelief and dismay he felt, she broke into a short run towards him. A second later they were in each other's arms.

'Darling Sarah!' stammered Frank. 'Wh-what...' He held her by the shoulders and looked into her face intently, as though trying to convince himself it really was Sarah. 'What are you doing here? I don't understand ...'

'I know. I know, Frank. Oh, it's so good to see you.' She pulled herself close to him and leaned her face against his shoulder.

Suddenly they were conscious that people were staring at them. Sarah blushed and this, together with the excitement in her flashing blue eyes, set a kind of fire alight within him.

'Look,' he said. 'Let's ... Can you get out of this place this evening?'

Both started to speak at the same time and then, amidst the confusion of their own voices, they were laughing. Yes, yes, she would try to get out. Where should they go? It didn't really matter. Anywhere ...

In minutes Sarah had thrown on her outdoor clothes and seated herself behind him, astride the motor-cycle. Frank headed towards Cassel. God knew what kind of revelry might be possible in such a place, but at least they were—unbelievably—together. There was the power of the bike beneath him and the quickening thrill of her arms about him; he revelled in the sense of protection he felt towards her. All the misery of the weeks before had gone by the time they reached the thickening confusion of the little town's main street on that early April evening.

Frank knew nothing of the place, but when he saw the somewhat dingy façade of the Hotel Normandie that seemed to be appropriate enough. They dismounted, laughing, and parked the motor-cycle in a little alleyway alongside the hotel.

Frank couldn't believe it all, and kept on telling her so until she placed a hand on his lips as they entered what appeared to be the hotel's dining-room.

'It's true,' she said softly. 'I'm here. I really am here, Frank.'

Madame—it was always Madame at that time of day—appeared to soften at the sight of the young flier and the nursing Sister. She actually smiled as Frank turned to her and asked if they could have a table.

Monsieur could certainly have a table, and as Madame tucked them away and they sat facing each other in a kind of daze, a young girl who could have been the woman's child appeared with a carafe of the local wine. Without waiting, Frank filled their glasses and raised his own to Sarah.

'To us,' he said, looking into her eyes.

'Frank . . .' A flicker of sadness swept over her face. 'Frank, I . . .'

'What?'

'I hope I haven't done wrong——'

'Done wrong? What do you mean?'

'Being with you again like this.'

'I don't understand,' said Frank, staring at her.

'But didn't you get my message?'

'I didn't know it was you. I just knew that someone from this hospital had been calling me all day yesterday. I thought it was to do with a dental appointment.'

'You mean you didn't know, when you got to the hospital, that I was there?'

'No.'

'Dear Frank.' She reached out to him across the table.

Dear Frank. Didn't he detect something like a trace of

pity in her voice?

When their omelettes arrived they ate hungrily, as though the process of eating could in some way quell the restless excitement they felt. He was about to ask her about the letter she had written when she interrupted him; almost as though she instinctively sensed what he was going to say.

'How long do you have?' she asked.

'Just tonight,' he told her. He related how he had come to pick up the aircraft.

'Is it . . . is it very frightening?' she asked.

'Not really. I love flying.'

'I know, but the danger——'

He leaned towards her. 'Sarah, why did you call me after writing that letter?'

'I'm sorry. I know I shouldn't have done. But it seemed wrong; being so near and not seeing you. Can't we not talk about it? I know what I said in my letter, Frank; still I think I was right. But there's no reason why we shouldn't be friends, is there?' She added: 'Shall we talk about it?'

'Not now,' he said.

'Very well.'

Frank ordered brandy. There was a sudden embarrassment in sitting opposite her this way, as though everything he had ever felt about her was there on display for everyone in the place to stare at derisively. She didn't seem to understand that she couldn't shift at will from friend to lover and back again. He wanted to say this, and when he had tasted the warm glow of his first brandy he almost did say it.

Sarah refused to drink. She had to be back by ten, she said, and there was the possibility that she might have to take over someone's night duty. But she sat there while Frank drank; so pristine, almost glacial in her blonde beauty. Recurrently he wanted to touch her, but he knew that would be wrong.

Steadily he drank cognac while they evaded the responsibility of saying anything that might touch too sensitive a chord. They talked of home, and of her parents' concern when she had announced that she was coming to France.

'Frank,' she said presently. 'You're drinking much more

than you used to.'

'Only on nights like this. Only when I'm celebrating . . . our *friendship*.' In spite of himself he put an emphasis on the word which was vaguely ironical.

He knew he shouldn't have done. She reached out to him. 'I *was* wrong,' she said quietly. 'I shouldn't have telephoned you.'

'No, you weren't wrong.' There was suddenly nothing more that could be said. He looked at his watch and told her that if she had to be back by ten, they should leave now. The evening was over.

He rode back with something less than the care he had used earlier, for the drink was having its effect.

'Goodnight, Frank. It's been wonderful.'

'Yes.'

Hurriedly she reached forward and kissed him on the cheek. 'Frank . . .' she began tentatively.

'Yes?' His voice was a little aloof, even impersonal.

'Will I see you again?'

'Of course. If you want to.'

'Take care of yourself, Frank—for me.'

'Of course.'

She was smiling as he turned back to the borrowed motor-cycle and then, with much revving of the engine, whirled off.

Damn, Frank thought as he drove as fast as he dared in the darkness towards the road which would take him back to St. Omer, why couldn't he be like Delaney? It was obvious that Delaney could handle women in a way that he himself would never be able to do. It had all been so help-less. Sarah, sitting there throughout the evening, so near and yet so unobtainable. Blast her! Why had she called him? And why had he been such a bloody fool as to go to that hospital?

The evening ended in the strange neutrality of the Mess to which he had been allocated at the base. He knew no one and was glad. There was an attempt to get up some kind of thrash, but these fellows did not have the necessary close-ness to whip up the right spirit. Frank went to bed in disgust when he felt he had taken enough brandy to make him sleep.

The new Pup was a beauty, delightful to handle. All the way back to the Squadron he threw her around the sky, sometimes savagely and then, as though in recompense, with the delicacy that might be used on a fresh young horse. Ten miles from home, when he could see the lake, he opened the throttle and really pushed her down.

Then at zero feet he skipped across country as though all the power in the world were his. Up then with the throttle wide open so that the Pup screamed in protest until he had reached two, three thousand feet. He was right above the Squadron's base now. Cut, nose back—now he would really discover if she would stay in one piece—until the stall. Kick. Rudder and stick hard over to the left so that she whipped viciously into the spin. His head reeled. The whole earth was spinning around its axis. Once, twice around. Then he caught the Pup with opposite rudder, pushed the stick hard forward and opened his throttle again. She surged back under control and came out at about a thousand feet.

He was on the downwind leg now, so he cut off power before heading into the last gliding turn. Now he could see that most of the Squadron must have been airborne. There were very few aircraft around. In a long, slipping glide Frank let down until he levelled out with his tail well down, and touched.

The usual attentive ground-crew ran towards his wing-tips, and when he had cut his throttle and climbed out, they couldn't wait to tell him—the Squadron had gone, or most of it.

Frank couldn't believe it. He ran to the Adjutant's office. Was it true? he demanded.

Yes, it was. Captain Gemmell, the ageing, taciturn Scotsman who ran the Squadron administratively, was a harassed man. He explained that most of the Squadron had taken off on the day before, at a couple of hours' notice, for an airfield behind the Arras Front. It was a temporary move; they would no doubt be coming back, but meanwhile their purpose down there presumably would be to help out with the battle that was taking place at that very moment.

Captain Gemmell asked Frank if he could assemble just after lunch, at two o'clock. Meanwhile, if he could have his batman pack an emergency kit, it would be picked up and driven to the new place by tender.

This would be a different kind of war, and Frank knew it as he hurried towards his billet.

CHAPTER SIX

There were four aircraft in the flight that took off that afternoon. Frank Thompson had been selected to lead. They had been briefed to fly to an aerodrome about five miles south of Arras on the Arras–Bapaume road. More than that the Adjutant was not able to tell him, for—as he confessed—everything had happened so quickly on the day before that he had been unable to get much information. But it was obvious that there was some kind of flap on.

Half an hour after take-off, the four Pups were flying at less than five hundred feet as Frank desperately scanned the landscape ahead in search of the aerodrome that had been described to him by the Adjutant. Ever since take-off the conditions had been difficult. Low, scattered cloud which had been bringing rain showers throughout the morning had been scudding across the field, and in other circumstances it was likely that the flight would have been cancelled. But on this day they had to go.

The distance to the new field was just over forty miles. Frank wasn't too worried about the map-reading, for with a flight of only half an hour there would be plenty of endurance left at the other end if there was a need to search for their destination. But he found the place without too much difficulty. They were low, though, around a height of only three hundred feet, and Frank was worried about the others as he waved them down into the strange field. One of these lads, named Crosby, had a total flying experience of seventeen and a half hours, so he had learned just before take-off.

But they made it, and the other three were already emerging from their Pups as Frank taxi-ed up to them. Young Crosby had an expression of such satisfaction on his face that one might have thought he had shot down the great Baron himself.

Major Simpson was there to greet them. He welcomed Frank's friendly salute with an outstretched hand.

'Frank, good to see you. How's the new Pup?'

'Splendid, sir.'

'Good.' The Major turned to the others. 'Gentlemen, there'll be a briefing later this afternoon. I'd appreciate it if you would stay in the Mess so that you can be contacted easily.'

'What's going on, sir? This was a hurried move.'

'Well . . .' The Major began to explain. Apparently pressure on the Squadrons already on this front had been very great throughout the previous week. He did not disguise the fact from Frank. Losses had been so heavy that it had been necessary to move four Squadrons of fighters, of which their own had been one, down from the Northern sector. And this kind of fighting would be different from the high-level patrols they had been used to. Down here most of their activity would involve trench strafing.

Delaney was in the Mess when Frank got there with the C.O. He'd just heard that America had entered the war at last on the side of the Allies, and he was in great good form. Large drinks were indicated and then, when Uncle Sam had been duly honoured, Delaney asked about the trip to St. Omer. Had Frank gone to the hospital?

For a moment Frank hovered on the brink of telling his friend what had happened. Then he changed his mind. Maybe he would tell him later. But not then. So he lied; he had not gone to the hospital, he said.

'You're a fool. Jeez, I don't know . . . First chance we get, Frankie, I'm goin' to have you in Paris and teach you something about women. Not London—Paris!'

To turn his friend away from the subject of women, Frank asked about the Squadron's function in this new move. But Delaney knew nothing. They had been ordered here on the day before. Most of the ground-crew hadn't arrived yet, which was why, Delaney supposed, there had not been a patrol of any kind that day. But that was all he knew.

After tea they were assembled in the Mess before Major Simpson. The Major seemed to be repressing an excitement

65

which he seldom betrayed. There was a hesitation in his voice.

'Gentlemen, as you can imagine . . . we have not been brought down here for nothing . . .'

There was some mild laughter from the gathered pilots.

'No, chaps, I want to be serious,' the Old Man went on. 'We are here to give immediate close support to the Army Corps on this Front, which means'—he had again to raise his voice above the hum of suppressed comment—'which means bombing, trench strafing, in short to cause as much alarm and despondency among the enemy's defending infantry as we can. To say nothing of the destruction we hope to inflict . . .'

He went on to announce that the first offensive patrol of six aircraft in three sections of two would take off that afternoon, in an hour's time.

Frank Thompson was glad of the imminence of action. He was to fly with young Crosby, the boy he had brought south that morning; so as their aircraft were being got ready he had a long talk with the boy, without generating anything like alarm.

Fleetingly, as he climbed aboard his aircraft to warm it up, Frank's mind reverted to the previous evening. He felt for a moment as though he could almost reach out and touch Sarah. Then his fitter was calling to him and the Pup trembled to the life of the engine. He was another man.

Crosby was on his right as they taxi-ed out. They were both carrying two small bombs, which had been fitted to their lower mainplane. The target they had been assigned to attack was a railway siding some six miles behind the enemy's lines at which he was disgorging, according to Allied Intelligence, reinforcements for his hard-pressed battalions. Frank's responsibility was to see that they found this place. But failing that the job would be to find and use discretion as to another secondary target.

The weather had cleared as they took off into the late afternoon, and within minutes they were flying at something like five hundred feet over the British Front. From that height it was possible to see the upturned faces of the Tommies below, and Frank felt that sudden twinge of fellowship which he always felt when he looked down on them.

66

The Front in this sector, so he had been warned, was somewhat confused, for the action of the previous weeks had to some extent been indecisive. As a result of massive effort and the loss of thousands of lives, a few hundred yards had been gained here and there; often only to be relinquished when it was discovered that enemy pressure was so great that the ground could not be held.

Once, as Frank raced the Pup towards the German lines, he heard a peculiar 'whish' very close to him as he did so there was a bucking of the aircraft. What the hell could that have been? he wondered. A shell? That was it—a shell and probably one of our own. He had heard of aircraft being struck by an invisible shell, and suddenly he pushed his nose down; for it could have been that at that height, around five hundred feet, he was in the line of trajectory.

Young Crosby followed as they dropped lower, and once Frank waved to him in encouragement. Quietly, as he looked across at that other aircraft and thought of the in-experience of the boy who was flying it, he felt a sudden rage at those who had sent him out. Then he was over what could now clearly be discerned as German-held trenches, and he dropped, looking quickly at the map which was strapped to his knee as he endeavoured to keep on track for the railway siding which was their target.

Now the natives were beginning to display their hostility. From somewhere ahead of them an ambitious group of Hun Archies was taking an interest in their approach, but to no avail. They were much too low, and getting lower all the time.

Frank fired a short burst on his gun, in the general direction of Hunland, but at nothing in particular. At this height there was no danger of the air temperature affecting their efficiency, but it was always good to know before you committed yourself that you were not suffering from any sort of jamming.

Down now to know the peculiar thrill of being like cavalry in full charge. Young Crosby was on his starboard and slightly behind. If this was their new style of operation it was already fun. Frank lined himself up on a road which he estimated would lead him just south of the siding they were to attack. This was the tricky part.

They were flying so low that any deviation from the immediate business of handling the aircraft was dangerous. But still he had to be sure that he turned off the three miles to the north which would take him over the siding at the right time.

Much more enemy activity was now visible, although it appeared that Jerry was developing some kind of early warning system against low-flying fighters.

Frank left the road and swung south around a wood with Crosby on his starboard, still following. They came suddenly on what looked like some scattered companies of field-grey figures and for the first time Frank fired a long burst into their midst.

Immediately there was retaliation. Individual Huns returned his attentions with rifle fire which he knew was not to be underestimated as a danger. And suddenly, when it was too late to be really effective—for the two Pups had swung around the wood and were on the scattered troops before it was fully realised they were there—machine-gun fire came from the ground.

Frank started to weave wildly, hoping that young Crosby was taking the same precautions. Then he was over the startled Huns and heading on around to port so that he came back on the road. A quick swing of the head told him that the youngster was still there, following his leader.

Frank had to guess at the turning north and he turned when the slender line of the canal he had been looking for came into view. It was a long time since Frank had dropped bombs and apart from that he suddenly realised how quickly the racks which held his two twenty-pounders had been fitted to the new Pup. He only hoped that the release gear would work, for the thought of trying to land back at base with a half-released, unexploded bomb aboard was not comforting.

He pulled up now and saw that young Crosby followed suit. To be too low was inviting trouble from the blast of their own bombs—apart from that, it was necessary to get some perspective of their target.

It was there! Frank looked towards Crosby and waved, indicating that he had seen their destination. There was an acknowledgement. Now was the test—for it was certain that the place would have some kind of protection. And indeed it had!

From somewhere down there more than one machine-gun was firing at them. Frank began weaving and signalled the youngster on his right to get into line astern; an order which, as far as Frank could see at that moment, he obeyed.

He had the railway line firmly in view now, and could see the parallel steel tracing stretching far away to the east. But Frank decided on a change of plan. He swung, when those on the ground were firmly aware of the attack, hard to starboard and then in as steep a turn as he dared at that height—bearing in mind the fact of the inexperienced boy behind having to follow him—he swung around to port until he was lined up on the single track and heading west.

No train was in sight so if those at H.Q. who had briefed the exercise had imagined there would be, they had been wrong. The plan must surely be to drop his bombs where they would do as much damage to the track and sheds as possible.

Frank released his bombs from about a hundred feet and then, still conscious of the ground fire that was coming up at him, he swung hard away. Both bombs seemed to explode and then, as he caught glimpses of the explosion without being able to assess accurately the damage done, he caught sight of young Crosby out of the corner of his eye.

So far all seemed to be going well.

Holding his Pup in the steep bank to port, Frank then saw Crosby's bombs go. Great! The whole siding seemed to rock with the explosion, and Crosby too seemed to be in good shape. They were around now and heading east again. Frank decided to go on. They were about six miles inside enemy territory; there must be something else worthy of their attention, since they had taken the trouble to get this far.

He dropped again to almost zero feet and waved to young Crosby behind him to close up on the starboard. A mile east of the railway siding they came upon a kind of support road which at first looked to be empty, but which —when it suddenly emerged from a wood—was occupied by a marching column of field-grey uniforms. They scattered like frightened sheep as the two Pups were suddenly upon them.

Frank fired a long burst into the column as it broke. He could see men firing at him, and was aware of bullet-holes appearing in the fabric of his starboard wing. But at that speed he was suddenly over the column and gone.

Over open country the two Pups sped, for young Crosby was still holding on grimly to his leader. And it was then, when they were about five miles from the original target, that Frank saw the airfield. Two aircraft were taxi-ing towards take-off when he was first upon the place. For, no doubt, all of this sector had been alerted.

Without hesitation Frank dived on the moving Hun fighters which looked at a first quick glance to be Albatros. One seemed to be attempting a premature take-off as Frank fired. He could see his tracer reach out across the landing field, and as his bullets hit the first of the Huns, it seemed—like some hesitant, elderly dancer—to change its mind, then slowly topple and hit the deck. It started to burn as Frank tried to get in a shot at the other one.

He couldn't fire through his Aldis. There was no time for that. All he could do was to line up and hope for the best. The best would have been possible if he had still been carrying the bombs he'd dropped on the railway siding. For now he was streaking towards the hangars, and he could see the panic beneath him as mechanics tried to run for shelter and a group of stouter hearts pulled at an Albatros in an attempt to get it under cover.

Frank fired again, and now was conscious of the fire that was being directed at him. Red tracer was reaching up to him, so far without avail. At the last moment he pulled over the hangars and then turned steeply to his left. It was hard to tell what damage his one gun had done to the hangar area, but it was certain that he had hit some of those Huns.

Now it was time to go, for as he turned Frank was certain he saw an aircraft coming in from the west at about five hundred feet. Where the hell was young Crosby? Desperately Frank swung his neck in an attempt to see if the boy was still with him and then, with a quick lifting of the heart, he saw him.

Crosby had followed him over the hangars and was making a slow turn to his left in an attempt to follow. Poor

Crosby. This was a damned awkward situation to be in when you'd only had about twenty hours' solo experience in the air, all told.

The difficulty of coping with the Hun above him was now preoccupying Frank. But there was really only one thing to do. He had to climb towards them. He wished at that moment that he had been alone, for he would have cut and run, but the trouble was that young Crosby probably hadn't seen them—and if this were the case, then the boy would be a sitting target.

There were two Huns and obviously they were returning from a patrol to this, their base. Steadily Frank climbed towards them—at the same time trying to indicate to Crosby, who was by now well up on his starboard, that the damned things were there.

Frank rocked his wings in the gradual climb, and he could see his wing-man nodding with a kind of excitement, although whether or not this was an acknowledgement that he had received the message, it was impossible to tell.

Suddenly, to his consternation, Thompson saw the two German aircraft with whom he was now gradually closing, turn away. What could it mean?

They were turning not only away from the two Pups but from their own airfield. It couldn't mean that they were shirking a fight. All the advantage—coming in from the west as they were and from above—was theirs. But now these two were distinctly turning away and climbing fast. It could mean only one thing; they had completed a patrol and had come back to find their own airfield being attacked when they themselves had run out of ammunition!

Deciding that his first duty now was to get young Crosby back to their own base, Frank gave up his attempt to close with the two Huns. He dropped his starboard wings, having decided to cover the twenty miles between them and base at ground level. There might still be some pickings down there on the way home.

Crosby was still there and Frank felt a kind of thrill for the boy as he saw him. They were flying fast now, medium throttle, but with their noses down they were picking up a speed approaching a hundred and ten with the enemy's front directly ahead.

His gun was still functioning. All was well.

Perhaps four miles behind Hun lines, Frank saw an open staff car whose driver seemed to panic as he heard the approaching aircraft. For suddenly the thing left the road and careered straight through a thick hedge. There was no point in wasting ammunition there.

From beneath came considerable enemy fire. Field-grey figures were everywhere. But Frank flew on with his head tucked into his shoulders until he had reached the furthest back of their support trenches. Now his blood was well up. From that height he felt as though he were conducting a war all on his own. At the support trench he swung along it, firing as he went, and then—after he had used up about fifty rounds—he swung west again, to the next trench.

Crosby was still with him as they reached the Hun's front line, but now further back as though giving himself time to see what his leader would do next, which was wise. What Frank did was to fly this time north along the front-line trench.

He could see the huddled figures beneath and then he seemed to be looking down the barrel of a Spandau as one brave Hun gunner tried to get at him. It was into that gun that he fired the last of his ammunition. The gun was silenced.

Around to the east now, and home. There was no time to reload the gun, and as he approached his own lines Frank could only pray that no trigger-happy Tommy would think they were Hun aircraft.

Beneath, the pock-marked landscape was littered with shell-holes and the debris of the fighting that had taken place there in the past weeks. If man ever got to the moon, Frank thought, it must look something like this.

His goggles seemed to be misting, so he raised them to his forehead. There, suddenly beneath his wings, were the furthest forward of the British lines. With a feeling of jubilation Frank rocked his wings in greeting to the Tommies beneath. He could see a few of them waving to him and as he swept over he waved back in greeting.

To make it easier to find their new field, Frank pulled up now to well over a hundred feet. His neck swivelled as he searched behind for Crosby, and at first there was a moment of panic when he could see nothing of the other aircraft. Christ! Had he lost him?

Throttling back, he had started into a slow turn to the north when away below him, almost sheepishly holding close to the earth, he saw the outline of the other Pup. The boy was still there. Now it was home.

As Frank saw the rectangular wood which was the best marker for the new airfield, he was filled with relief. They had made it.

Around fast and in. The landing of both Pups was unspectacular. Somehow in the proceedings of the past hour there had been a difference. There had been nothing of the gladiatorial splendour of combat in the air. This had been a rigidly functional operation, and its nature was dictating the mood of both pilots. Frank taxi-ed up smartly with young Crosby following, and when he had silenced the engine and jumped out, he ran across to the other Pup. Young Crosby was beaming all over his fresh boy's face.

'Jolly good show,' congratulated Frank as he gripped the youngster's arm.

'Thank you, sir.' It was obvious that Crosby was pleased and exhilarated by his own performance.

'Don't call me sir,' Frank protested, laughing.

'Sorry, sir———'

They almost skipped to the hut in which the C.O. was waiting. But it was a grim-faced Major Simpson who greeted them.

'How was it?' he asked.

'Splendid, sir!' Young Crosby could hardly contain himself. He seemed to be totally unaware of the luck they had had and, as Frank said, 'used up'.

Major Simpson listened as Frank made his report, carefully emphasising what a splendid performance had been put up by the newcomer on his first op. It was only when Frank came to relate the two Albatros coming in from the west as they had been attacking the airfield, that Crosby let himself down. Frank was explaining to Major Simpson how alarmed he had been when he had seen the two planes come in above them, obviously on their way back from patrol, and he was emphasising their position before the two Huns inexplicably turned off, when Crosby said:

'Huns? What Huns? I didn't see anything ... Really I didn't!'

He blushed as the other two burst out laughing.

'That'll teach you, young Crosby,' Major Simpson said, laughing as he took the young man by the shoulder. He accepted the salutes of both men as they were about to take their leave.

Frank had reached the door of the hut when the Old Man checked him. 'Oh, Frank,' he said, 'can I have a word with you?'

Crosby hesitated.

'No,' Major Simpson went on. 'That's all for now, Crosby. I just want to have a word with Captain Thompson.'

As the door closed, Frank said: 'Sir?'

'Do you think that lad's fit to go out again?'

'He put up a first-class show, sir. If he ... if he's lucky he'll make a top-rate member of the Squadron. Of course he can go out again. I'll have him fly with me any time. In fact, it might be a good idea if he continues for a bit to fly with someone like myself or Delaney or one of the more experienced pilots.'

'I mean now.'

'Now, sir?'

'Yes, when you're refuelled and re-armed.'

'If it has to be done, sir. But I think it's damned hard ...'

'I know, I know. Frank, we lost the two A Flight aircraft on that show.' The Major spoke testily as though he were angry at having to use the words he had just spoken. As indeed he was.

There was a sharp rap at the door.

'Come in!'

It was Sergeant McFee who entered. He saluted smartly and then waited for the C.O. to speak.

'Yes, Sergeant?'

'Sir, it's Lieutenant Crosby's aeroplane——'

'What about it?'

'The engine, sir. Be u.s. for twenty-four hours. Two cylinders damaged by enemy action.'

'Crosby didn't mention anything——'

'He wouldn't know,' Frank put in.

'All right, Sergeant. Thank you.' McFee was dismissed and left the room with a flicker of a smile to Frank when he had saluted the Old Man.

'Well, that settles that, sir,' Frank said.

'I'm afraid so. You'll have to go it alone, Frank. I'm sorry.'

After a careful inspection of his own Pup, in the company of the faithful McFee, Frank took off on his second low-level operation of that day. The trip was uneventful enough. But that night when finally he found the seclusion of his own bed he sank into it as a man totally exhausted.

For hours after the end of that second lone patrol he had been sustained only by the nervous energy that had built up inside him. There was a kind of bliss in finally stretching out on the bed and he thought of nothing and nobody when he slipped into sleep.

And so it was for days. The Squadron was in action throughout the hours of daylight, constantly on call by Brigade or Corps Headquarters as the great land battles seethed to and fro, with no real degree of conclusion.

But the objective— and it was impossible for those taking part to know at the time—was being maintained. Further to the south, General Nivelle's offensive was coming to a grinding halt at immense cost to the French. Rumours were filtering through of mutiny in certain units of the French Army, and although these were being discounted by the troops, they were sufficient to cause some degree of alarm.

Arras could only be discounted as a failure in terms of ground gained, but as a means of relaxing pressure on the hard-pressed French further south, it had its element of success.

R.F.C. losses were reaching heights that the powers-that-be knew would be difficult, if not impossible, to sustain. Frank's Squadron had been cut in half with the roll of missing, killed and injured. Perhaps more seriously some of the better experienced pilots were among those missing. Seven pilots were lost in just over that number of days.

But, strangely enough, morale remained remarkably high. For all of them could *see* the battle in which they were taking part. Day after day as they swept across the lines like airborne cavalry, strafing, bombing, sending terror into the hearts of the enemy, there was the feeling of tremendous comradeship with those in whose support they flew.

It was Delaney who said to Frank one night in the Mess after dinner : 'How are you feeling? What's the war doing to you these days?'

'It's keeping me fit,' Frank said.

'Keeping you fit? It's driving me nuts!'

Frank laughed. Delaney went on to say : 'Naw, naw, isn't it strange? They've been flying the arse off us day after day and I get the feeling that people feel good. Even with the losses. Have you noticed?'

'Noticed what?'

'We haven't had a real thrash since we got down here.'

'There hasn't been time——'

'But we have now,' Delaney said. 'Hey, waiter!'

But it didn't work out that way on that particular evening. Instead the two men, with young Crosby—who had tagged on to Frank since the first patrol they had done together—decided to investigate the splendours of the Naval Squadron with which they were sharing the airfield. It was well known that the Navy had the best of everything, even in aircraft. For this particular unit was equipped with Sopwith Tri-planes, an aircraft not especially designed for ground strafing, but being used in that emergency. It was Frank's ambition to 'have a go' at a Tripehound, and this was one of the main reasons for agreeing to Delaney's suggestion.

The Naval pilots were a light-hearted lot and they eagerly welcomed the visitors. It would have been difficult, apart from the obvious uniform differences, for an outsider to have discerned any marked difference in these Naval pilots from Frank and his friends. Perhaps the most obvious was that they drank gin.

It was Delaney who pointed this out. He said, after they had been drinking for perhaps an hour, to one of the Naval group which was entertaining them : 'You guys all drink gin. Why is that?'

'Well, old boy,' the Naval man said with the easy elegance of his kind, 'it's like this. In the Navy the troops drink rum and look what happens to them when they get ashore——'

'They get drunk.'

'That's right. The officers drink gin, and that way we're usually in a condition which allows us to get them out of jug . . .'

Everyone laughed, and then again as Delaney suggested that the idea was so good he would have another gin. And all of them did, again and again, so that to their surprise, when they arrived back late at their own Mess, it was agreed that gin was a good idea. Even young Crosby was in good enough condition to suggest a fast game of table-tennis.

It was two days later that Frank, an hour before break-fast, on the first patrol of the day, was crossing the lines at five hundred feet. Again he had Crosby with him, for with-in a period of a little more than ten days the youngster had been sufficiently 'blooded' to rank as something of a veteran.

Above them there was a solid cloud mass. Visibility was poor, and was not at all helped by the mass of artillery smoke which was hanging around. They had hardly crossed the enemy lines when they ran into trouble.

Two Albatros—Scouts—came thundering out of the overcast and straight into them, firing fast.

Frank had rehearsed such an eventuality with young Crosby by this time. He gave the signal to break and the youngster did so while his leader turned hard to port, hop-ing to draw the two Huns after him and away from the other Pup. There was no point in going down, so Frank gave the Rhone engine everything it had. Both Huns shot past on their way down while he stood virtually on his tail in an attempt to get into the safety of the heavy overcast.

God, the stuff was thick! Sudden panic seized Frank as he momentarily lost his sense of balance. At that angle of climb there was real danger that he might stall. He eased the stick forward, gently; the throttle was still wide open. He broke cloud and wondered momentarily as he did so if he were right side up. He seemed to be.

There was no sign of the two Albatros, but there was a sudden flurry of fire from the ground. He realised that he was now over the Hun lines. He pushed the nose down and left his throttle wide open as it had been for the climb.

The Pup had now been modified to take four twenty-pound bombs. She felt just a fraction sluggish with the extraneous objects hanging beneath the lower mainplanes.

His target was the airfield near Douai, just north of the River Scarpe. It was one of the German fields that were giving heavy support to the Hun Infantry in its efforts to hold off the Allied attacks.

Luckily the river made the target easier to find, and Frank smiled as he thought of how good landmarks near an airfield could be double-edged blessings.

He was surprised when he saw no sign of young Crosby as he neared the Hun airfield. He hoped to God those two Albatros pilots had not jumped him.

The last vestiges of the early dawn were disappearing as he made his first run. The first bomb he dropped on what he later described in his report as 'the second shed from the east'. It was a hit! He could see the panic beneath him.

He turned then and swung steeply around until he could make a run at another shed. Again he scored a hit. This was marvellous and once more he swung around to make a run. Another shed seemed to be hit. There was one bomb left, but as he made his run the damned thing wouldn't release. He cursed.

Below, all was confusion. There was some desultory firing, but nothing that as yet could be described as serious. Now he would have a go with his Lewis.

But where the hell was Crosby? The boy should have been on the scene by now. There was no sign of him. Damn! Frank pressed his Bowden control as he swung around yet again in an attempt to make a really low run across the field. There was a quick stutter of fire, then nothing.

Like a man possessed Frank hammered at the gun, to the point of forgetting how low he was. For suddenly there was a thump as he touched the grass of the Hun airfield. He pressed the Bowden again as he bounced and it fired. Incredible! He had touched at something like a hundred and twenty miles an hour—and he was still airborne.

Frank fired everything he had into those burning sheds, and then when he was up and over he saw what he took to be two Hun officers exercising their horses. So in a near stall turn he swung around until he could have a crack at them—which he did until the terrified horses bolted. There was a great thrill in the morning. As he roared over those scampering horses Frank was laughing within himself.

Once right around the airfield Frank swung the Pup and then across it towards the west—which had in retrospect been rather silly, for they were now gathering their wits sufficiently to mount the beginnings of a reaction to his attack. But Frank's blood was up. Somehow there was a commitment that morning which he had not felt of previous days.

He opened his throttle a little more fully, pressed forward gently on the stick until he was down again to a height of something like thirty feet and raced for the Hun's front-line defences.

The first of the morning's real light was behind him. Beneath he could see hundreds of individual smoke columns as the Hun infantry prepared its breakfast. Here and there he saw a scattering of figures as he suddenly swept over them. There was no suggestion of any ground fire being directed at him, so he sped on without undue anxiety. Perhaps it was the time of day that made him feel as he did. There was the thought that because he was so early the advantage was all his—which in a way it was.

Frank tested his gun as he approached their rearmost trench. All was well. So he turned steeply to his left and swept along it, pouring a long burst into it. Men—and the trench seemed to contain comparatively few of them— threw themselves against its sides in terror. One machine-gun bay seemed to be in action and quickly Frank swung on to it without taking time for any deliberate aim. He simply sprayed fire in the general direction of the gun. He thought he had got it but then—damn!—there was a sudden hard jolting as the Pup was hit. Again he swung to the west, conscious now of the exposed belly of the Pup.

There were two more lines of Hun defences to cross, and as he headed for them he wondered how badly he had been damaged. At first things did not seem too bad. Then the engine began to surge wildly. His heart kept unison with its unsteady roaring. He couldn't think. All he could do was freeze himself into a kind of prayer which told him to go on and keep his head down—something it was impossible to do in the confines of the tiny Pup.

Now came the next trench, across which he stumbled rather than flew. There was rifle fire from the now alerted Huns. He gave them a burst and then became vaguely aware of the fact that his gun was no longer firing. Again he was hit, but this time there was the sensation of wetness in his thigh. He must have been struck . . .

He cursed as he tore on. He had been a bloody fool. He should, after his success with the bombs at their airfield, have climbed to some kind of height which made sense. He tried now to gain as much height as was possible as he crossed their front line. But by now the whole German Army seemed to be having a go at him. There was no point in trying to hit back. All he could do was fly on and hope that his machine would keep going until he reached his own lines.

It was a forlorn hope. A burst of what must have been machine-gun fire ripped through the fuselage. His instrument panel suddenly seemed to disintegrate. Furiously he tried to weave the aeroplane. How high was he? In a kind of panic he threw back the goggles from his eyes in an attempt to ascertain how far he might be from his own lines. But it was impossible to tell.

Suddenly his engine died a juddering death. There was something wrong, too, with his hand. His right hand.

There was only one thing for it—he would have to stretch his glide as far as he could and hope that the Pup could take him as near to the British lines as would give him a chance to get home.

Beneath, the prospect looked bleak. The earth had been churned with the passage of the recent fighting. He would be lucky if he could get the Pup down without breaking his neck!

Frank weaved on down. There was no airspeed indicator left to tell him how close to stalling speed he was stretching the Pup. But the light was good. His leg now felt very wet; he wondered how badly he had been wounded. Damn! He could feel the glove on his right hand getting sticky with blood. Ease down! To stall even from that height would have been crucial, so Frank once more eased the stick forward. He was too fast as his head went from side to side in an effort to see what was ahead of him. Back on the stick, gently as he could, for the right hand was now stinging sharply.

He was down suddenly.

It was impossible to tell what was happening. He seemed

to touch with the tail well down and then trundle forward
and drop. That was all Frank knew. At the time he was
quite unaware of climbing from the cockpit and looking up
at the rim of the biggest crater he had ever seen.

CHAPTER SEVEN

The sun was well above the eastern rim of the crater in which he found himself when Frank stirred.

Where was he?

It was only then, when he was asking himself the question, that he was aware of the noise. Crazily, for some moments he wondered if he were dead and that this was what it was like to be dead.

There was the broken aircraft. His Pup, nose-down in this great hole in the earth with only its tailplain possibly showing above the rim of the crater into which he had fallen.

At first Frank pressed himself back against the wall of the crater, his mind and his whole being filled with fear. He looked at the sky and as he did so clamped both hands over his ears to shut out the crescendo of noise.

Something stirred and he stared in disbelief. He could see that it was a rat, then came another and another. Where the hell was he? He could feel his glove sticking to his right hand and there was pain above the knee of his right leg, too. He tried to move the limb and found he could do so without too much effort.

Everything around him he saw with a kind of disbelief, and in those first moments he had to force himself to make an effort, to struggle to remember the sequence of events which had brought him to this pass. He looked at his watch. He must have been unconscious for a couple of hours, for it was now almost 9 a.m.

If that was the case, then the tremendous noise which was filling the world around him must be that of a pre-attack bombardment. He was between the lines. He remembered that now. But if someone *was* about to attack— then who?

It had to be the British. For weeks now they had been on the offensive. If it wasn't, to be caught there could well mean that his war was over.

The Pup would never fly again. For one thing, it would be impossible to retrieve it from this position between the lines, and even if an advance meant that rescue crews could get here the poor old Pup looked as though she had well and truly broken her back.

There was one thing, though—the dashboard watch. Those watches were valuable, and if his was still serviceable there was no reason why he should leave it for the first Tommy or Hun who came this way. Frank moved and then cursed himself for a fool. There were more important things than watches to be thought of at that moment—like survival. He decided to climb the wall of the projecting crater and try to discover what there might be in the world outside.

To climb through the mud of the crater would not have been easy even in normal circumstances, but in Frank's present condition it was especially difficult. He was perhaps half-way to the top when something of the almighty din which had brought him back to consciousness seemed to be dispelled. His heart beat more quickly. What could it mean?

Then came the sound of whistles. Vaguely at first he heard them; then unmistakeably he was listening to the signal for an infantry attack. He climbed on, impervious to the danger; right then his curiosity was the instinct which over-rode everything else.

One glimpse was enough. With only his eyes above the rim of the crater he could see the first of the straggling figures, laden with the accoutrements of attack, climbing from the trenches to the west of him. He slid back down the wall of the crater. God, what should he do?

To expose himself now to his own infantry would have been madness. Frank slid on down until he was again half-crouching at the base of his funk-hole. These people must have seen him come down. All he could suppose was that, with the imminence of an attack, they hadn't dared risk sending anyone out to pull him in.

He'd been lucky. At that moment, as he waited for the first of the attacking Tommies to storm over and around him, he was telling himself just how lucky he had been. If the crater in which he had landed had not been as deep as in fact it was, if his aircraft had been more visible to the Hun, then they would surely have attempted to shell it to destruction and he would certainly never have come back to consciousness.

Frank cursed the stiffness of his right hand. He loosened his fur-lined flying jacket, for a sweat was now gathering on his body. A cigarette; he must have one in the tunic he wore underneath . . .

Now machine-gun fire—presumably from the German trenches—was biting through the morning air. It was a steady rat-a-tat-tat, steady and remorseless. Now he heard voices, occasional cries of frightened men.

'Steady!' he heard someone cry out. 'Steady——'

Who were these men now threading their way through the mud towards the enemy he would probably never know. There was a sudden stirring within him as he thought that he should not be cringing in that hole. It wasn't good enough. He should have been up there with them. It was a foolish thought; he knew that. But it was there and it stayed with him so that he moved his legs restlessly against the wall of his muddy prison.

It was strange to be there, a witness almost to the attack. As it went over him he was aware only of the sporadic shouting, the scream of the artillery offensive now lifted further to the east, the crazy rattling of machine-gun fire. The human involvement of which Frank could be aware as he cringed in that hole was almost something superficially imposed on the mechanics of the battle.

In quick succession there was the explosion of three heavy shells close by. The Hun was now aware of the attack and was retaliating murderously. Frank buried his face in the earth and was aware suddenly of its comfort. There was no comfort in the sky.

In minutes—certainly not more than five or six—there came again the cry of voices. Was this another wave? It was, and then there was a confusion of noise—much cursing, the animal cry now and then of a man's agony. God, how long would he have to stay in this damned hole?

Frank was thinking of his Squadron now, his people at home. A report of his being shot down must by this time have reached Base. He had been missing for hours. It would no doubt have been different if he hadn't chosen to crash in no-man's-land a couple of hours before an impending attack. But as it was, he must be presumed missing by the Squadron. In as much time again Signals would be being prepared about his death.

The earth was churned now by the retaliating Hun artillery. The whole of creation in those moments seemed to have disintegrated into whirling chaos. It would have been different had he been taking part, had he been exposed or consumed with the latent anger which can propel a man in action. But lying there, helplessly, he could only be a mute witness.

Frank leapt at a sound above him and saw the figure of a soldier tumble into the crater. His heart thumped at the sudden violence of the man's appearance. And then, as the intruder gathered himself up from the heap in which he had fallen and became aware of Frank's presence and the unexpectedness of his appearance in his heavy, fur-lined flying jacket, he reached for the bayoneted rifle which had fallen from his grasp. In the same instant Frank jumped him.

There was desperation in the move, for instinctively Frank knew that the man, in his state of confusion, was dangerous. Somehow he got a foot on to the rifle and then, as the soldier tried with a kind of hysterical gesture to strike him, he called out :

'Easy, chum, easy !'

'What . . . what . . . Christ !'

The poor devil was shaking with shock.

'All right now. Easy,' said Frank.

The man was searching his face and then looking away from him towards the crashed Pup. Something like a vestige of understanding crossed his face and he sank back against the wall of the crater, emitting a long heavy sigh.

Poor devil, thought Frank. The man closed his eyes then wiped at his mouth with the back of his hand.

'Christ !' he said again.

'What's happening?' asked Frank.

'Hopeless . . . bloody hopeless.' The accent had the unmistakeable rhythm of Lowland Scotland. 'They've got new wire out there that our lot didn't know about. The gunners couldn't have known about it either. It's all broken

85

down . . .' The man began to shake as though with ague.

'Here——' Frank reached with his left hand into the pocket of his tunic and brought out a crumpled pack of cigarettes.

'Thanks, Jock.' The soldier lit up and drew heavily on the cigarette.

'Are you hurt?' Frank asked.

'I don't think so.'

Frank saw the man's water-bottle and was suddenly aware that he was terribly thirsty. The man saw the direction of his gaze and offered the bottle to him, then drank himself. It was then he realised who Frank might be.

'I'm sorry, sir,' he said. 'I didn't realise you were an officer. Did you come down in this thing?' He gestured towards the Pup.

'I'm afraid so . . .'

'We saw you falling. We all thought you were a goner. Nobody could come out for you; we were all standing by for the attack. That was why——'

'Do you think we should try to make it back for our lines now?' Frank asked.

The man shook his head. 'If you put your head up there, chances are you'll not have it for five seconds. We're on the run.'

He had hardly finished speaking when again there was a flurry above them and another figure reached the edge of the crater and tumbled down its side. Frank saw that the man was an officer. He carried only a revolver and looked as though he had been wounded.

The Scotsman seemed to know him for he went over and as the officer was struggling to get to his feet, he helped him. But it was hopeless. The newcomer was obviously badly hurt.

'Who is he?' Frank asked.

'Lieutenant Morrison, sir. He's from our A Company.'

Frank forgot the stiffness in his right hand and the pain in his thigh. He struggled through the mud across the crater floor until he reached the wounded officer.

'Give me your water-bottle,' he said to Jock. The man did so, and Frank sprinkled some of the contents into the officer's mouth.

'Thanks . . . thanks,' the man mumbled. 'Look, don't stay

here. We're falling back on our own lines. The ... the attack's failed. They may counter-attack. If they do we're done for here——'

'Can you move?' Frank asked.

'I don't know.'

'Let me look at you.'

When Frank was able to examine the officer he found that the shrapnel of machine-gun fire had ripped his left knee almost to pieces.

'I got it, just there ... Just there I got it!'

'I know, old man. Don't worry. We'll get you back. Take it easy now.' Frank spoke reassuringly, but his heart was heavy. There was a whole long day of fighting ahead of them perhaps, and this man needed immediate attention. God alone knew what condition he would be in if they had to wait twelve hours or more for darkness. He must be taken in now. But above them came always the scream of shells and the rattle of angry machine-gun fire.

Frank turned to the soldier at his side. 'Jock, we've got to get this man back now,' he said.

'Couldnae we wait a wee bit, sir? Till it's kind of died doon?'

'No. It'll be more dangerous then. We should try now, in the confusion. Look, get hold of him and let's try to get him out of here. How far do you reckon it is to our lines from here?'

'Maybe fifty yards, sir.'

'Give me a hand with him.'

As they took hold of the wounded officer he gave a sharp cry of agony. Frank apologised. 'Sorry, old chap. Sorry about that. We'll try not to hurt you. But if we're going to get you back I'm afraid we'll have to.'

The Scotsman was strong and now, with the reassurance of Frank's authority, he seemed to be feeling much stronger. The pair of them, Frank and the infantryman, half carried the wounded officer up the walls of that muddy crater until they were able to see over the edge.

Everywhere men were straggling back across no-man's-land. It was an incredible sight. All the activity, the half-running, crouching men, was so unco-ordinated. There seemed to be no plan to anything that was happening—as indeed at that moment of time, there wasn't.

87

Frank waited. He had one last look at the Pup, lying there with its engine deeply buried in the mud and its back broken. He felt as though there were some kind of treachery in leaving it there.

The officer was breathing heavily, every now and then emitting a sharp little cry of pain.

'Hold tight, old man,' Frank said, trying to be as reassuring as possible. 'We'll soon have you out of this place. Ready, Jock?'

'Ready, sir.'

'Let's go then. Keep your backside down as much as possible——'

'Don't worry, sir, I will ...' The Scotsman grinned through the coating of mud on his face.

The wounded man was game. It was his left knee which had been shattered, and he was crawling as much as he could on his right side. They went on, and now it seemed as though they were alone on the field of battle, for the whole tide of retreat had swept back to their own lines. But the firing had been more sporadic. Frank was praying that the confusion in the Hun lines would be such that for the time being they would be able to make as much headway as possible before the enemy reorganised himself.

On now, on ... Propelling themselves as they were on an elbow and a leg, the going was slow. For Frank it was even more difficult, for his right leg and hand were now beginning to give him hell.

When the shell screamed above them Frank's experience was not enough to tell him of the danger. But the Scotsman shouted a quick warning.

'Down, sir!'

It landed close. For a moment Frank was sure they had been buried alive, for a great shower of earth and slimy water seemed to envelop them. He held to the body of the wounded officer and when the world—or those few feet of it through which they were crawling—became still again, he moved.

'All right?'

The officer made some sound which seemed to indicate that he was, but there was nothing from the Scotsman.

'All right, Jock?' asked Frank anxiously.

Still there came no reply.

Frank released his hold on the wounded officer and crawled around his body until he found the infantryman. Jock was quite still. Frank shook him. Almost incredulously he said again : 'Are you all right, Jock?'

But Jock was not all right. He made no movement at all, and he made no sound. He was dead. The faint trickle of blood from his mouth told all that there was to tell.

Now there was a kind of desperation in their plight.

'How is he?' the officer asked.

'Dead.'

'Leave him then. Let's get out of here!'

They crawled on. Frank half dragged the other man. Now and then there was a burst of fire from behind them as the Hun swept no-man's-land irritably. From ahead there were the first signs of the British front line being reorganised. Occasional rifle fire crackled out. Then the barrage came again.

Someone must have asked for additional artillery support to keep the Hun pinned down in his own trenches. For as they crawled slowly on there was a mighty screaming of shells above their heads.

'How are you doing?' Frank asked the Lieutenant.

There was a long pause before the man answered. Then he said, with no conviction at all : 'All right . . . I think.'

But it was obvious to Frank that his charge was in a bad way, crawling painfully across the rutted ground. He himself felt for a moment as though his own strength was going, but with the feeling there came a tenseness of will that seemed to impel him on.

Now the sun was rising high above them. There had been an early morning mist, but with the heat this was clearing. If they didn't get in soon there would be little chance of getting in until darkness.

How he covered those last yards until he heard their voices, Frank never knew. It was possible that he himself was in a near coma. There was no pain in him now, and the effort of dragging the other man had become part of the rhythm of his body.

At first there was something like a threat in the sound of the harsh Scottish accents. Frank was afraid to call out lest the trigger-happy—and no doubt by now, jittery—Jocks decided that anything that moved or made a sound was a worthy target.

'Heh, lend us a hand, will you?' Frank called out at last. His voice was hoarse now from the efforts he had made and the enforced thirst of the last hours.

'Who's that?'

'Friend.' It was all Frank could think of to say. 'I've got one of your officers here. Lend us a hand, will you?'

Two of them came out and when they reached Frank hardly a word was said except: 'Come on, Jock, you've only got about ten yards to go. Get your arse in gear!' The words were spoken with a truculent irreverence that was alien to Frank.

But the invocation worked. He seemed to find a new source of energy and with one of the men who had come out to them—a boy, rather, for there was something in the lad's movements and sense of urgency which seemed to express extreme youth.

Frank was in the forward trench, and a minute later half a dozen men were helping to lower their wounded officer. They had made it.

An officer bustled up and instructed the men to bring Frank and the wounded officer to a dugout further long the trench. When they had reached its shelter and cautiously edged down the sloping steps the officer, who introduced himself as Captain Macintosh, apologised. They were rather busy at that moment, for they were expecting the Hun to launch a counter-attack. He gave Frank a large tot of whisky and pointed to the bottle which stood on the crude wooden box serving as a table.

'Help yourself if you need some more,' he said.

Frank thanked him and sat down, gratefully.

'We saw you come down this morning. I'm sorry we couldn't get someone out to you. We were on stand-by and afraid that any activity on our part might give Jerry some idea of our intentions.' Then he laughed wryly. He was a young man of about Frank's own age, but it was obvious that he had been through a great deal that morning. 'As it happened, our caution didn't do us much good, I'm afraid.' He paused, and looked at Frank more closely. 'Are you hurt?' he asked.

'My leg, I think,' Frank said. 'And this hand——' He held

up his right hand.

Two ambulance men were detailed to attend to him. They managed to get his glove off eventually and then they removed his boot, ripped his trousers, and applied a field dressing to his leg. The leg wound was superficial, a lot of blood but nothing very serious; but the hand they thought might need more expert attention.

Whistling again indicated that the men in the trenches above were being alerted. Frank prodded the two men applying their dressings to hurry. They pinned his trouser leg together and he removed his helmet, flying jacket and the boot from his undamaged leg. He felt mobile again, and as he did so the claustrophobic oppression of that dugout seemed to move in on him. He had to get out into the morning air. Perhaps he had been flying too long. Perhaps because the sky had become his battlefield the idea of being caught in that hole in the ground had terrors for him that probably existed for no one else there.

He climbed back into the trench. Men were manning the firing step, each at the ready. Someone who appeared to be a Major came running along the trench, extolling his men to steadiness. He looked at Frank as though he were some creature from another world, but hurried on.

Someone's rifle—no doubt someone who had been a casualty of that morning's attack—was lying against the parapet, so Frank took it and examined it for fitness. There was nothing wrong with the gun. He decided to have a go himself on the firing step and as best he could he climbed up between two Jocks, who turned to look at him in astonishment.

They saw the wings on his tunic and the pips on his shoulders. It was incomprehensible to them. One of them thought to say : 'You've got no steel helmet, sir.'

'I know,' said Frank. 'We don't use them where I come from.'

Looking along the barrel of that rifle was a reassurance. 'Do you think they'll come?' Frank asked the man on his right.

'No, sir.'

'Why not?'

'It's too late now. If they'd been coming they'd have been here half an hour ago.'

But the man was wrong. Perhaps the Hun should have listened to his kind of wisdom. But suddenly, out of the smoke that was creeping across the mud separating the lines, the first of a force of perhaps battalion strength was coming at them.

An officer shouted: 'Hold it! Don't waste your fire!'

This was another war. Here there was no relation to the swirling combat that Frank had known even that very morning in the air. He was in a static battle now. Men were lurching towards them through the almost impassable mud; men alongside him waited for the moment when their fire would be most effective.

Machine-guns chattered on the word of command:
'Fire!'

The Jocks fired as one man. Now it was their turn. An hour before it had been they who had lurched across that hell out there. Now there was revenge in each of their trigger fingers.

This was no massive onslaught. Field-grey uniforms did not approach shoulder to shoulder like some great human juggernaut. These men had had a bellyful that morning. They approached half running at the crouch, bayonets fixed.

Rapid fire swept like a tornado from the rifles along the trench in which Frank stood. He suddenly found himself enjoying the heat of this new role. Unlike the fighting with which he was familiar there was the consolation of Mother Earth, the smell of the men on either side, their curses; and when it became apparent that Jerry was breaking under the sudden and impressive onslaught that came at him from a light artillery battery behind, there was a sense of sharing the experience which was alien to Frank.

Men began to cheer hoarsely. Perhaps they were watching their own fears recede. But it was obvious now that the back of the attempted counter-move was broken. A few brave Germans got quite far before they were cut down. One man—a huge fellow who must either have been half crazed or had the heart of two men—came on at them although he must have been hit half a dozen times. He lay moaning for a long time, crying out in an incomprehensible agony for death to relieve his suffering.

Frank jumped down from the firing step when it

appeared that it was all over. He jumped, in fact, almost into the arms of a Major who seemed to be the Company Commander. The Major was beaming.

'Hello,' he said. 'I heard we had a visitor. How the hell did you fire that rifle with that hand of yours?'

'I didn't.'

'No?'

'But I was going to have a damned good go if anyone of those characters had got close enough to fire at *me*.'

The Major laughed and introduced himself. 'My name is Kinross,' he said. 'I'm commanding this Company—what's left of it.'

Frank said: 'I'm Thompson.'

'Yes, I know. I'm sorry we couldn't do more for you this morning, but I'm sure you realise the position. I'd like to say how much I appreciate what you did for Lieutenant Morrison, the man you brought in. Is there anything I can do for you?'

'If it's possible to have something to eat I'd be very glad,' said Frank.

'Of course.' Major Kinross was a rather jovial, thick-set man of about twenty-seven. In spite of what his Company had been through that morning there was little evidence of anything like battle-fatigue in the Major's attitude.

At Company Headquarters Frank wolfed happily into some bacon they had brought him. There was more whisky flowing, and as each of the officers drifted in and was introduced to him, the atmosphere of an 'occasion' seemed to build up.

Whisky appeared to be in fairly plentiful supply with these Scotsmen and in spite of the morning's repulse and the losses they had sustained, their spirits were high. Perhaps the holding of that half-hearted counter-attack had helped.

There was no possibility, the Major said, of Frank's getting away from them right then. But they were being relieved at dusk that day; he could go back with them then. Meanwhile they would try—although without much hope, for at Battalion there would be chaos after the events of the morning—to get a message back that would reach his Squadron.

In a way it was fun to settle in with the routine of an infantry battalion in front-line duty. They treated him as some kind of celebrity, asking all sorts of questions about his Corps, doing a good deal of drinking. In fact, so much so that by the time dusk had fallen and they were ready to move out, Frank was feeling little of the pain of that day.

For three miles the remnants of the Scots Battalion trudged back through the gathering darkness. They had been relieved by a Northumberland command. They were tired; some of them had lost friends that day, and there was much grumbling and cursing when they saw the tents into which they were to be consigned for the night. But the cooks had been busy and there was the inevitable stew with carrots to eat. At least it was hot.

The officers fared little better. Major Kinross found a tent which Frank could share with him. They made the semblance of a Company Mess. There was at least the whisky.

But now they could relax. Once or twice the phone rang for the Major, but in the main they were resting. Drink flowed. Much toasting was done to the honour of the Royal Flying Corps. In return, Frank drank to their Division, their Regiment, their Battalion, their Company.

Eventually it was time to sleep and he crept gratefully beneath the ground-sheet they had given him. It had been a long day. When he had taken off that morning, dawn was not yet a reality. What the hell had happened to that kid Crosby who had taken off with him?

There was a final thought, and he was almost asleep when it came to him. The watch. Before he had left that crater he should have looked again at the Pup's cockpit to see if the watch was still serviceable.

Damn!

CHAPTER EIGHT

Back at Le Hammeau, the Squadron had been detailed to return to its own base in the Northern sector and as always, their full kit had only just arrived, after two weeks.

The M.O. was somewhat concerned about Frank's hand. There was no doubt that the wound was in need of some slight but fairly intricate surgery. His leg would heal easily, but the hand was in need of attention.

To have this done in this particular sector would have been awkward. It meant that he would have to find his way back to the Squadron in the North afterwards. Then the Adjutant came up with a solution—a Nieuport two-seater was going back to St. Omer for modification and Frank could fly as the passenger. He could then make his way to the hospital at St. Marie-Cappel, and when he was fit travel back the twenty miles to Base. They would send a tender for him when he was ready.

In the make-shift Mess Frank was discussing the some-what protracted trip he was about to make on the following day with Delaney—who had been delighted to see his friend back. Suddenly he saw young Crosby.

'Ah!' said Frank, laughing with relief. 'What happened to you?'

'I'm sorry, Frank. It's good to see you back. I hear you had a ghastly trip——'

'Ghastly! It was nothing,' Frank said. 'Why didn't you stay with me? You could have joined the fun.'

'I'm ... I'm awfully sorry.' The two men laughed at the now blushing Crosby. 'Frank, when those two Huns attacked us on the way across and you went into cloud, I lost you and then I got lost. I couldn't find that airfield——'

The boy was genuinely contrite. 'I'm terribly sorry,

Frank,' he apologised again.

'Shut up!' Delaney plied him with a drink. 'You didn't get lost on the way home. That's what matters. We love you, sonny boy. We like having you around.'

Crosby made some excuse about having letters to write and was gone as quickly as decency would allow.

'So . . . it's back to that woman of yours at the hospital?' said Delaney to Frank.

'It looks like it.'

'The fates are working for somebody, that's for sure.'

Frank did not reply, although the same thought had been in his own mind. He had thought of trying to talk his way out of the arrangement, but there had been something—the pull of Sarah, perhaps—which had silenced him.

When he arrived at the hospital after the flight in the back of the old Nieuport two-seater to St. Omer and then the dreary journey by tender to the hospital, he reported quite officially. For there was still the lingering thought that perhaps he could go there and leave without seeing her.

The operation on his hand was performed on the day of his arrival in the afternoon, and Frank had believed he could walk straight out of the hospital afterwards. But the doctor who had stitched the wound was insistent that he should spend at least one night there.

It was after supper on that first evening that Sarah came into the ward. She walked straight to Frank's bed and when she saw him there a look of disbelief came to her face.

'Frank!'

He smiled at her. 'Yes, it's me. I thought you'd be surprised.'

'Are you badly hurt? What's wrong——'

'Nothing serious. They were just patching me up a little . . .'

She leaned over and kissed him on the cheek. 'I couldn't believe it. I almost died when I saw your name. Oh, Frank——' She took him by the shoulders and held him more warmly than he had ever known her to do.

'It's all right, Sarah. Really, there's nothing to worry about. I got caught in a spot of trouble yesterday—or the day before. It's nothing, really . . .'

'But what *is* wrong?' She was still looking concerned.

'My hand—my trigger hand, unfortunately. And a

scratch on the leg. Nothing——'

'Couldn't we ... Do you feel strong enough to get up, Frank? Come to my room; I have a friend there. We can talk and have a drink. Oh, this is wonderful!'

He raised his eyebrows in pretended irony.

'Oh, I don't mean it's wonderful to have you wounded,' she hastened to correct herself. 'I mean, it's wonderful that if you have to be in hospital, you're *here*. That's what I mean, darling.'

He thrilled to hear that 'darling'. He reached for the dressing-gown that hung by his bed, got up and put it on. Three other officers were in the tiny ward, but they were either asleep or drugged. He was the only casualty. But when Sarah tried to help him he said, a trifle impatiently: 'No, it's all right. It really is nothing.'

In Sarah's room there was another girl, another Sister who stood politely when Frank entered. Sarah introduced them, and after the preliminary small talk the girl asked if they would excuse her. There was so much she had to do at that moment.

'Drink, Frank?' Sarah asked when the door had closed behind the girl.

'Drinks,' Frank said, smiling. 'I didn't think nursing sisters ran to such giddy heights of depravity.' He smiled because he had decided that, after their last meeting when it had all descended into such depths of utter, hopeless seriousness from which neither had been able to extricate themselves, it wouldn't be that way again.

They drank the Scotch she poured and he told them about the Scotsmen he had been with for two days. It made their being together easier to be able to talk about something. But suddenly she broke off.

'Frank,' she said suddenly. 'I'm sorry about last time——'

'It's ... al-alright.' He stumbled over the words.

'It's not all right. I behaved like a silly little girl who needed spanking.' She paused then went on: 'Frank, I'm sorry about that letter. It's not easy for me to say this—I know you love me, and I think—I know—I'm sure I love you. But that isn't enough ...'

'What else is there?'

'There's so much more ... Getting married means more

than just being in love.'

'Not these days,' said Frank gruffly.

'I don't . . . I don't feel——'

'You mean you don't feel you want to marry me?'

'It isn't that. It's my father. And your people. You know they were keen on our engagement, but they all felt we weren't in a position to get married.'

'What does your father know about being in love? Or my people, for that matter? They're all old. They've forgotten what it means to be in love.'

'It isn't only that——' She looked away from him, confused and unhappy.

Frank was remorseless. 'What is it then?' he demanded.

'I couldn't bear to hurt Daddy.'

'He hurt us.'

'He didn't mean to, Frank. He admires you and all that you are doing. I know that. But he's already been hurt once——'

'Your brother?'

'Yes. Daddy never says much, but I know how dreadfully cut up he was about Jeremy's disappearance. All those gambling debts, and the women . . . Not coming back for the war . . .'

Frank sipped quietly at his drink, looking at her above the rim of his glass. Sometimes, and especially in that uniform, she could look so exquisitely beautiful that something in him seemed to melt as he looked at her.

'I think,' she went on, 'that it would break Daddy up completely if I went against his wishes. I'm all he's got now.'

There was nothing he could say. She reached out to him and touched his arm. Then she smiled with a weary resignation.

'I shouldn't talk like this,' she said. 'Here you are, wounded—you could have been killed!'

'It isn't much of a wound.' His voice was tense, a little edgy and she knew why. Suddenly she moved forward and was in his arms, looking up at him. Her pale face glistened with tears.

'Oh, Frank, what are we to do?' she cried. 'What are we to do?'

'There's nothing to do, is there?' he said and his voice still held a remoteness which hurt her more than any words could have done.

Next morning Frank was shattered when he received a signal from the Squadron's Adjutant. He was not to return to the Squadron. He was instead to proceed on home leave and await posting.

He couldn't believe it. Home leave! It was only a little more than a month since he had come out from England. Something must be wrong.

As soon as possible he got through on the telephone to Squadron Headquarters. They eventually found the Adjutant for him, but a full two minutes passed before the man could calm Frank down sufficiently to make him listen.

'Thompson, will you *please* listen to me?'

'But I don't want any bloody leave!'

'Look here——'

'I tell you, I don't want to go home. I've only j-just got b-back out here!' As always, in moments of stress or emotion Frank's stammer betrayed him.

'Listen——'

'Am I being grounded or something?'

'For God's sake, man—*listen*!' The Adjutant's angry tone finally penetrated Frank's mood.

He apologised. 'I'm sorry, but——'

'Look, Thompson, how long will it be before your hand is better?'

'Only a matter of a few days.'

'That's not what the doctor told me. It'll be a week or more, he said. You're virtually convalescent. What are you going to do, hanging around here, even if that were possible?'

'What do you mean—possible?'

The Adjutant paused a moment, then went on: 'I want you to go to England, not primarily to be on leave, but since your hand is at the moment useless, you might as well rest it at home. Now . . .' the Adjutant had raised his voice in anticipation of Frank interrupting him again, '. . . when you're at home you will receive instructions as to where you will rejoin the Squadron. Now calm down do, there's a good chap. I really cannot say any more over this damned telephone.'

Frank was silenced. England. Home. Leave. What did it all mean? Off he went to see the doctor who had stitched up his hand; a decent enough fellow, who told Frank that in a couple of days, when it was seen how the wound was responding to treatment, he could go home.

Two days left in which to be with Sarah! Oh God, thought Frank miserably, if only Delaney had been with him to advise him. Frank himself was filled always with a sense of reverence towards the girl, almost as though she had been his best friend's sister.

In the hours they could be together—for the hospital was engaged in a great flurry of preparation for the offensive on that part of the Front about which everybody was talking —they walked in the hospital grounds or in the quiet lanes surrounding them. Over those hours Sarah changed from the girl he had known in England. It was not that she said anything which was directly in conflict with her previous decision, but there was something in her mood which puzzled him. He couldn't think what it was until on the afternoon of the day before he was due to leave, he saw her walking in the grounds and talking to some of the men who had been her patients. It could be, he thought, suddenly, that the suffering she had witnessed among these men had made her more aware of the unimportance of their own lives.

On the night before he left they went to the Café in Cassel where they had had that first meal which had been so disastrous. This time Sarah had arranged transport so that she and a girl called Penny, who seemed to have some kind of London society background but in spite of her affectations was quite good company, trundled into the village in an ambulance driven by Penny. With them was a gunner, a Captain Calderwood. It was the first time Frank had ever been driven by a woman and he was genuinely surprised that such a thing was possible.

When Sarah had first suggested that they make up a four-some he had been disappointed, but in the end he had to admit that it was as well the other two were there. Penny was very amusing, with a faintly biting wit which tickled Frank, and she and Captain Calderwood went to great lengths to make the evening as gay as possible.

They rollicked back to the hospital in immense form. There was nothing left of their previous tension; but Frank experienced a tender warmth in being with Sarah and he could tell that she felt the same way.

Captain Calderwood insisted that they take back some bottles which they had managed to prise loose from Madame, and they did. When they had parked the ambulance the bottles were smuggled into Sarah's room, to the accompaniment of much giggling from the two girls.

From somewhere a gramophone was produced, and they drank and sang quietly—at least, almost quietly, for the two men were occasionally tempted to break into louder tones. They even danced in the tiny space, and while Frank was dancing with Penny she said suddenly:

'You're in love with her, aren't you?'

Frank said nothing. The words of the song—'*If you were the only girl in the world*' ran through his head, intensified by the drink he had taken.

'I don't think this is a time for being in love,' Penny went on, in no way abashed by his silence.

'Don't you?' Frank's voice was noncommittal.

'No. But it'll be all right in time. You'll see.'

Frank did not ask her what she meant. The rest of the evening melted with the aroma of the cognac. Somewhere along the line Penny and Captain Calderwood left. Frank and Sarah continued to dance, again and again, to the music from the same rather worn record; but he did not remember much about it, or of falling asleep on Sarah's bed and waking up three hours later to find her dozing on the rather uncomfortable armchair.

She guided him back to his own ward, praying as they went along the corridor, that they would not meet anybody in authority. Nor did they.

Next day Frank was driven to St. Omer and from there towards the night-boat from Calais. It was just after lunch on the following day when he arrived at 'The Grange'.

His parents were delighted to see him and—as he had feared—his mother made a tremendous fuss over his wounded hand, which was still bandaged. Over the next few days of waiting he walked, and spent a lot of time talking with his friends who were still at home. Not his contemporaries, of course; there were none left by now. But it was still fun talking with the farmers who had allowed him in the old days to shoot over their land.

He waited for eight days and one afternoon, as he arrived home for tea, his mother met him in great excitement. A telegram had arrived for him.

When he opened it he saw that it contained instructions to present himself at a place called Hayling Green, in Kent. He presumed this must be an aerodrome. But what the devil were they playing at?

That evening he walked through the village with his father. They talked of his brother Harry and of the progress he was making with his job on the Staff. But Frank detected less heart in the Old Man than he had ever done before. It wasn't exactly a pessimism, but there was something in his father's attitude which seemed to suggest that, no matter who the victor was in this war—which had already lasted so long—nothing would ever be quite the same again.

All these new people coming to the fore . . . Everything would be different. They would not too easily relinquish the power they had found for themselves during the years of war.

CHAPTER NINE

Hayling Green was, in fact, an airfield, so Frank discovered with relief when the cab which he had taken from Dartford had finally arrived at the front gate of the place.

But—more important—as they approached Frank saw a Pup in the circuit. And more important still, the guard on the gate informed him that his own Squadron was installed there.

Delaney was the first man he met in the Mess. There was great excitement and slapping of backs all round and so much babbling of voices that it was difficult for Frank to take it all in at first. But eventually Delaney was able to drag him away and he was able to get the gist of what was happening.

Apparently the Squadron, with one other, had been seconded temporarily to Home Defence duties. Nothing was being said in the Press, but it seemed that recent daylight raids by the Huns' latest heavy bomber, the Gotha, was causing considerable alarm among the powers-that-be, to say nothing of the populace itself. Something had to be done, and it looked as though this was the High Command's 'sop' to Parliament and public opinion.

Frank was thrilled. It might be fun to have a crack at the Hun heavies, but there was even better news. For night flying the Squadron was to be given three Camels while it was on the Home Defence job. Camels!

Training began immediately. As a matter of fact, it was the first chance the Squadron had really had to train as a unit. By day Frank was leading his old B Flight, for his appointment as B Flight Commander had now been officially gazetted by Wing. Half a dozen pilots, Frank and Delaney among them, were allocated to night-flying, training on the new Camels.

For hour after hour Major Simpson had them practising tight formation flying on the Pups, and it was particularly cheering to the more experienced pilots that the youngsters should be given such a chance. Even if they never saw a Gotha, this flying experience would be valuable when they got back to France.

For even in the short time that Frank had been away, there were more new faces with the Squadron than he would have cared to see. Losses on the Arras 'do' had been heavy and it was beginning to be rumoured that losses throughout the Corps in the past month had been the heaviest of the entire war. The Squadron had lost eight pilots killed in a month.

Still they practised on, and almost two weeks had passed. There was no sign of a Gotha alert; there was likewise no sign of the rumoured Camels.

Then one morning at breakfast when Frank and Delaney, together with young Crosby, were planning the possibility of a trip to London, great excitement stirred the Mess. Someone shouted that the Camels were in the circuit.

Everybody dashed out to watch the arrival of the new machines as they swept around the glistening airfield, fast and supremely confident.

They looked quite different from the Pup—whose 'big brother' they were, of course. The hump in the middle which was their guns had given them their name. But the wings looked different. They did not have the upswept dihedral of the Pup. Instead, the lower plane was exactly parallel with its upper. There was a squat tightness about the Camel; she looked strong.

That afternoon Frank was able to handle a Camel for the first time. He was delighted. The extra power was thrilling to use and the machine could turn on the proverbial sixpence. But best of all was the assurance he felt merely by sitting behind those two guns. God, if only the Squadron could be equipped with this machine in France! There was talk that they would have them soon, but presently they would be heading into high summer and if events ran true to form it would be winter before they saw them on active service.

Major Simpson had agreed that if weather was suitable,

Frank and Delaney could have a go at flying the Camel that evening when darkness came.

But by dinner-time the weather was closing in, and by the time they had eaten it was clear that there would be no flying that night.

Perhaps it was just as well. Over the next two days there was the opportunity to handle the Camel until both of them began to feel really at home. They were now on constant patrol of the Kent coast twice a day, on the look-out for enemy bombers. They flew high, but nothing happened. There began to be talk around the Squadron that nothing ever would. Some of the pessimists were saying that their presence in England was merely a token gesture to the politicians. Hun intelligence, too, must have been aware of their presence.

When Major Simpson strolled into the Mess one afternoon at tea, on their return from their second patrol of the day, and announced that night-flying was 'on' for that night, Frank and Delaney laughed politely.

The Old Man understood. 'I know, I know,' he said. 'But it really does look as though you'll be able to have a crack at them tonight.'

Frank was due to go first—just a few circuits of the airfield to get the feel of flying at night, and then down; these were his instructions. He decided he would have dinner when he returned, and when he was asked why he wasn't eating and told them he would do so later, they laughed.

Someone remarked: 'Be smart. Have your dinner, old boy. Remember the condemned man and his breakfast . . .'

There were few men in that Mess who would not gladly have preferred to take off on a trench-strafing patrol over the Western Front rather than take an aircraft off the ground at night. Already they had produced the aphorism: 'Only owls and fools fly at night.'

But Frank, although tensed up, was not especially apprehensive. He had tried to rationalise the situation. He was now a pilot of considerable experience. There were problems in night-flying because of the crudeness of the instruments as yet available, but there would be a moon and consequently a horizon. There shouldn't be too much difficulty.

'All right, chum!' Delaney called as they walked out to the waiting aircraft. The sun had just gone; in fact, conditions were perfect. There was little wind and what there was of it was in the right direction for take-off and landing.

Delaney added: 'Don't forget—if the bloody Hun can fly at night, so can we.'

'Correct,' nodded Frank.

'I'll buy you a treble Scotch if you don't bounce more than three times on the first landing.'

'There's only going to be one landing,' Frank said. Then he added: 'I'll buy you a bottle of Scotch if you don't break the Camel!'

Both of them inspected the waiting Camel in which Frank was to fly. Then he climbed aboard. On his right he could see the flickering row of paraffin lamps which would guide him into the air—half a dozen frail torches against all the immensity of darkness around them.

He had settled himself in the cockpit when the C.O. arrived to say a last word.

Frank pulled back the flap of his helmet as he leaned towards the Major. 'Sir?'

'Frank, I want you to take it easy this first time.'

'Yes, sir.'

'One circuit will be enough. Just get the feel of the dark, then make a landing. That's all I want you to do.'

'I understand, sir.'

The Major looked at him keenly. 'Now, I mean that, Frank——'

'Yes, sir.'

The Major stepped back and as he did so Frank called to the ground-crew: 'Contact!'

A couple of swings and the engine roared into life. There was the feeling of real power as he caught it with his throttle. What a difference from all the string-bags he had flown in the past couple of years! The Pup was a fine little aeroplane, but this was something different altogether. This was a military machine, and it felt angry.

He taxi-ed towards the glims. There was a strange new sensation of being more alone than he had ever been before. That was the thing with night-flying. By day there was the familiarity of the known world; but this was a strange other world. The darkness had obliterated everything familiar and known.

At the end of the glims, a man with a green Aldis lamp flashed it in Frank's direction. All was now clear for take-off.

The Camel trundled on and then Frank turned her until he was facing along the line of flickering lights. He revved up until the power pulled him forward. He was off with the slipstream screaming past his ears.

Tail up, and now the torque was exerting considerable pull. He fought hard on the rudder, but he had her. Now gathering speed he knew he had control of the torque and opened his throttle fully. She was roaring down the line of glims now.

One thought was imprinted on Frank's brain—*Don't look back at the lights*. No matter what happened he mustn't do that. He had been told time and time again that it was the surest way to spin in.

At around sixty the Camel was airborne. But still he held her nose down; it was safer to have as much airspeed in hand as possible.

Frank flew straight up. He had reached around a thousand feet before he started his turn to port, slowly, in a very flat bank.

On the take-off run there had been a fair horizon, but now as he slowly turned on to a reciprocal course there was almost none. God, it was dark! He looked down to port where the lights should have been, but there was nothing. He flew on, holding her straight and level. His airspeed was ninety miles an hour now.

His watch! He realised that if he flew on this course for a half-minute he should be at the down wind end of the field. He did that and then turned rather nervously to port again, when he should have been able to see something of the half down glim lamps. As yet there was nothing.

From the cross-wind leg he turned again straight into wind. He had seen nothing, but there was no need to panic. This time he would make a wider sweep, and he would relax. In an effort to do so he released somewhat his hold on the stick.

Into the wind there was again the horizon. For a moment, looking towards the high bank of cirrus which was obscuring the moon, he thought he saw something of the sea in the far distance. Guessing, he turned again across wind, and then down until he estimated he was once more back at the down-wind end of the field.

It was then that, beneath his port wings, he saw the lights. Something of a mild shock clutched at his heart and instinctively he cut the throttle. His height was still in the region of a thousand feet and he should really have gone around again. But having found the lights this time he was determined to go in on them.

Eerily the Camel slipped down in the night. She was fast losing height, for while not exactly side-slipping he had overshot the lights and had to weave back towards them. A rather steep bank back to starboard, then again to port. He was high as he approached what he imagined to be the edge of the field. Undoubtedly he should have gone around again, but there was in him a sudden desire to be on the ground. Just to be down once, to touch the earth again—then he felt he would be ready to take off for ever. But right then he wanted to feel the reassurance of *terra firma*.

He felt it all right, for when he hit about a third of the way along the primitive flare-path, he did so with a re-sounding thump which he was certain must have pulled the undercarriage off. Instinctively his left hand gunned on the throttle to cushion with power his return to earth. He was lucky. The Camel settled, tail down, with all the hesitant concern of its namesake settling on sand. She ran along the grass until she came to a rather breathless halt. It didn't seem as though anything were broken, thought Frank—nevertheless, it was the worst landing he had ever made!

When he had taxi-ed back to the hangar Frank climbed out of the Camel as sheepishly as any kid might have done after his first solo. As soon as he switched off he could hear Delaney's laughter.

'Say, do you owe me a treble Scotch!'

But nothing was damaged and as they always said—if you could walk away from it, it was a good landing.

Frank decided not to watch Delaney when he made his first attempt at night-flying. He ate dinner instead.

An hour had passed and Delaney survived his first night solo. They were at the Mess bar, comparing notes, when Frank was called to the telephone.

It was the C.O.

'Frank, Major Simpson here—could you get hold of Delaney and bring him over to my office immediately?'

A somewhat agitated C.O. was awaiting them when they reached his office. At first Frank thought he was in for some kind of a rocket as a result of the landing he had made, but it wasn't that. There was apparently some Zeppelin activity expected over London and the Home Counties—no one knew yet how serious it was. The first of them had been reported over the Estuary ten minutes before.

The Major was sorry, for he realised they had just made their very first night solo, but it was for this reason that they had been brought back from the Front. The Squadron should, if at all possible, make its contribution. How did they feel?

Immediately both Frank and Delaney leapt to the bait. Of course they would have a go at the Zepp. Were their Camels properly armed? It seemed that they were.

The Major was conciliatory. 'Now look,' he said, 'I know that darkness tended to fox you both this evening. But I've a feeling it was because you were only flying at circuit height. When you get to operational height on a night like this it should be much easier.'

They agreed, and ten minutes later both were climbing in a great arc towards the north-east. Neither could see the other, but the Major had been right. Beneath them was an outline of the south-east coast, which was almost as clear as it might have been by daylight.

According to the information they had received the enemy was flying at something in the region of fifteen thousand feet, but there was no reliable way of confirming it. Frank flew on. He flew as far north as London, and it was evident from the flashes he could see that there was some activity there. Searchlights scanned the sky like weird witches' fingers. Frank flew towards them, but it was hopeless; he could see nothing.

For perhaps twenty minutes he groped around in the night sky over London, but it was not until he had decided to complete one more circuit of the city before heading for home that he saw the Zeppelin.

Searchlights had been flickering across the sky and Frank, heading west and slightly to the north from the ribbon of the Thames—which he could see far below—was flying towards a cluster of lights when out of the darkness he suddenly saw the sinister great shape. It was about three thousand feet above him and to the west.

Immediately Frank fired his twin guns, and was startled at the strength of the recoil. It hadn't occurred to him that the extra gun would have such an effect. For a moment he felt as though the Camel would fall over backwards.

At full throttle he was reaching up for that massive black shape as fast as the Camel would climb. Now the 'Archies' were becoming active and he realised that the closer he got to his would-be prey the greater was his own danger of catching some of the shrapnel.

As it was, he was on a converging course with the huge Zeppelin, which now appeared to be heading for the coast. Frank's plan was to climb and turn so that he was behind and, if possible, above it.

The Zepp swept right overhead, and as it did so he was appalled at the size of the monster. So much so that as he strained his head back to look at it, he was afraid in some idiotic way that the thing would hear him. In the darkness, in the immensity of the sky, there was something almost primeval in his fear.

When he turned until he was on a following course, the Zeppelin was still a thousand feet above him. But he was closing and still gaining height in the sturdy Camel. Damn those searchlights! There was the sudden fear in him that one of them would envelop and blind him. He edged a little to his right.

Then it all happened, and there was a kind of horror in the happening. Frank actually saw the little F.E.2 above the giant—for that was what he took it to be. He saw its tracer and then he saw the four explosions literally rock the great, cigar-shaped monster.

For a moment he felt a pang of pity. The huge, lumbering sky-beast was helpless. At that moment he didn't think about the men in it; it was simply a vast, throbbing animal which was experiencing a pain it couldn't understand.

When it exploded Frank swung off to starboard into the sheltering darkness and from there he saw it fall. Great waves of flame billowed forth and then, some half-way towards the earth, the monster broke in two like something totally stricken.

For about ten minutes Frank flew around in a wide arc watching far below him the burning Zeppelin. He himself had had nothing to do with its destruction, but there was a deep satisfaction in having been so close to the event. Now all he had to do was to find his base and get the Camel down in one piece.

CHAPTER TEN

It had been the Savoy, and then the Café Royal, but neither seemed to fit the needs of their mood. Delaney was looking for action and when Frank and young Crosby asked him to define what he meant by 'action' he could only repeat: 'You know—action!'

The three of them—Frank, Crosby and Delaney—were sampling the delights of town. Champagne cocktails had been consumed at the Savoy, much gin at the Café Royal; for it was Delaney's conviction that before a man ate he should drink gin, and after he ate, brandy or Scotch. The other two were willing to believe him while they waited for the pheasant they had ordered.

'Well now, fellas, this is what I call the life.'

Delaney was in splendid form. He loved the rich, plush interior of the room in which they were sitting, with its mirrors reflecting the radiant lights.

'Gee,' he went on. 'Why can't it be that a man can come to a place like this every night? When this goddam war is over I'm going to find me a bank to rob, and then I'm going to spend the rest of my days just living it up like this. I am, you bet!'

They had eaten their pheasant and were tasting the first of their brandy when Frank told Delaney about this very place in which they were sitting—for all he knew, the same room—being where Oscar Wilde had held court in the nineties.

'You mean,' Delaney asked incredulously, 'The guy all the fuss was about?'

'Yes. He was a very great writer——'

'A *writer*?'

'Don't look so astonished. He was one of the greatest

conversationalists of his age. Frank Harris once said——'

'What the hell do I care about these guys? D'you mean we're sitting in some kind of fag's hangout?' There was an expression of disgust on Delaney's face.

Frank was puzzled. 'Fag?' he repeated. The word was unfamiliar to him.

Delaney did not elucidate, but ordered another large brandy instead. If folk didn't know what a fag was, he wasn't going to waste time telling them. They would, he decided, go on to Daly's.

In the London of that time there was a sensual appreciation of the city's delights. Every evening was spent as though it were the last. Even those who were in no way as exposed to the vagaries of fortune as Frank and his two friends seemed to appreciate that no matter what happened their world would never be the same again. As a result they grabbed greedily at the pleasures they were offered.

The show at Daly's was of little interest to Delaney. He knew that every girl in the world was the only girl in the world. So they drank. When the girls joined them, young Crosby was only slightly more nonplussed than Frank, but he did his eager best.

The eldest of the three girls singled out Crosby. She was a pleasant enough wench, but her boldness would have embarrassed Frank, who had still never succeeded in quite losing his natural diffidence where women were concerned. Delaney singled himself off with the blonde; it appeared that blondes were an American predilection.

The third of the girls was a rather shy, dark girl, perhaps a little younger than Frank. Her looks gave the impression that she could have been of partial Italian extraction. It took some minutes to realise this; in fact, it was not until he had spoken to her that Frank realised she was indeed quite beautiful.

She asked if they were on leave, and Frank hesitantly said : 'More or less.' That was the end of their initial conversation. He asked her if she would care for a drink, and when he said it she looked towards the bar with an expression on her face that required no words. She was given a drink.

In fifteen minutes Delaney and Crosby had paired off with the other two girls. The party had been split up. Frank now found himself more or less alone with the girl whose name he had not quite caught when she had first introduced herself.

In the end he asked it again, and the stammer was back in his voice.

'You d-did tell me,' he said. 'But I'm afraid I've f-forgotten. My name is F-Frank . . .'

'I know,' the girl said. 'Mine is Steve.'

'Steve?' Frank's eyebrows shot up.

'Short for Stephanie. My father always called me Steve. I think perhaps it was because he always wanted a boy.'

She smiled and when she did there was a warmth in her that Frank didn't believe could exist in someone who was a comparative stranger.

'Please let me get you another drink,' he said.

It was only when she remarked that he appeared to have lost his friends, that he realised Crosby and Delaney had gone. He wanted to remain with her, yet he knew that he shouldn't. In the end he said, hesitantly :

'Shall we go somewhere else?'

'Do you know a place?'

There was something in her tone at that moment which seemed to relate him to all of the human race. But he told her he knew nothing of London.

'I'll get my coat,' she said.

As he waited for her he was aware of a growing fear that she might not come back. The kind of girl she was probably wanted somebody older or more sophisticated—or richer—than he was. He had ordered another drink and was finishing it, convinced now that she would not return, when he heard her voice at his elbow.

'Here I am. Ready?'

They seemed to know her well in the little bar to which she took him. The Irishman who served behind it called her 'Stevie' and was pleasant to them both. It pleased Frank, in some peculiar way, that they seemed to treat her with a natural respect.

Everything became suddenly easy. The Irishman—when he realised Frank was of the R.F.C.—refused to allow him to buy any of the drinks, which for a time was embarrassing until Steve whispered to him that it would be wrong to refuse the hospitality. The confidence seemed to bind them

114

closer together.

He took her from the place as a natural consequence of their being together. There was no awkwardness. She didn't ask him. They simply left and took a cab to the address she gave the driver.

Even when they arrived at her place—by which time Frank was wrapped in the pleasant glow of the evening's alcohol, there was no embarrassment.

They drank again in her room, she to his continued good luck and he, somewhat drunkenly, to their continued friendship. She made coffee and when they had drunk it and smoked a cigarette apiece, she undid his tunic. Then she slipped her arms beneath it, around his waist, and he took her in his arms.

'Oh, Stevie . . .' he muttered. 'Stevie . . .'

She undressed then and when she had done so, and was beckoning him from the narrow bed, he slipped off the rest of his clothes and got in alongside her.

All next morning, as he made his way alone back to Dartford, Frank tried to reconstruct the events of that night. He could remember the love-making and faint, sweet smell of the girl. He could remember sleeping and then waking and then making love again. He could remember so clearly.

It had been Stevie who woke him. 'Hey, pilot,' she had said gaily as she stroked his forehead to bring him out of sleep. 'Time to get up . . .'

She had made coffee while he dressed, and some toast, which he ate hungrily. Even when she had mentioned money she had done so as though the discussion were between two old friends.

'Frank, do you think you could let me have a couple of pounds?' she had asked. 'I'm behind with my rent and it would be nice if I could pay off the landlady this week . . .'

Something in his subconscious told him that it was probably a stock phrase which she used to all her customers, but he did not care. He gave her five pounds and kissed her again before he left.

It was only when he was in the train that he began to relate the girl to the rest of his life. He looked out at the green countryside, lush with the bounty of early summer, and thought again about Sarah. How strange that she whom he loved and desired so much should be so many worlds away, physically and spiritually, when he was with her; and that this girl, this stranger, should have been so close!

CHAPTER ELEVEN

The flight back to France was conducted splendidly. Before crossing the Channel, the Squadron landed at Lympe, refuelled and then headed on its way, keeping perfect formation, without incident.

Now they were deep into that year's June. The Battle of Messines was about to start. Every available aircraft was required at the Front.

They were back now, three miles north of the River Lys, their nearest village being Merville. It was a pleasant enough spot, which they were sharing with a Squadron of Bristol two-seaters; friendly chaps in spite of the fact that the Squadron pulled something of a 'line' when making its first landing. In Flights, as they had been practising in England, they spun off into fours, pulled out, and then made rather smart formation landings which were executed without mishap.

It was not the kind of performance which is calculated to endear a new Squadron to one flying two-seaters which is, as it were, already in occupation.

It was on their second day there that news of Frank's M.C. came through.

Frank himself had been on line patrol with young Crosby. Two hours they had flown up and down their patrol line, which had taken them as far north as Polygon Wood and as far south as Lille. They were well over the Hun lines, but throughout the patrol they had seen nothing except some of their own aircraft.

The evening had been perfect, and on the way back to Base they had played like schoolboys. In the end Frank, with Crosby close on his starboard wing, had swept far west of Base until he found the hospital at St. Marie where

Sarah was working. Three times they flew around it at tree-top height before speeding back at the same height towards the south.

Both of them were laughing with pleasure when they climbed from their aircraft. But when Frank saw Sergeant McFee running towards him he realised that something was happening.

'Hello, Mac, what's the trouble?' he asked.

'It's no trouble, sir.' McFee was beaming broadly. 'I've just heard from the Orderly Room. Your M.C.'s come through!'

'My *what*?' demanded Frank, astounded.

'Your M.C., sir.'

Frank turned to Crosby. 'Did you hear that?' he asked. 'They've given me the M.C.——'

Young Crosby emitted the wild whoop of an Indian war-brave as he ran towards Frank to congratulate him. Then it was off to the Mess, where Delaney had organised a reception committee of somewhat unusual nature.

For when Frank and Crosby made a decidedly hurried entrance everyone there—and that meant practically every pilot on the Squadron—was standing in silent little groups with their backs turned towards the entrance. Young Crosby, as they entered, was about to call out; and indeed got as far as 'I say——' when Frank caught him by the arm, halting him.

He indicated to the boy to say nothing, and was walking with him to the bar, still enclosed by the total silence of the others, when the atmosphere was suddenly ripped apart by Delaney's voice.

'Hip, hip——' he cried, and the answering '*Hooray!*' almost lifted off the flimsy roof.

Then they were all around Frank, raising him shoulder-high and running with him around the ante-room as though making a 'lap of honour' on a football field.

There were de-baggings, a tremendous pitched battle in which the weapons were soda syphons; the bar was almost wrecked and finally the barman took refuge in the kitchen. The proceedings had settled down to a rather wild game of 'bunch, cuddy, hunch' when the Old Man arrived.

Gradually, as they realised he was there, the place became silent.

'Gentlemen . . .' There was no reproach in Major Simpson's voice. 'Gentlemen, if you will listen a moment I think you'll appreciate that there is even more noise outside than there is in here——'

Gradually they subsided, except one or two of the youngsters who babbled on to some extent on the fringes of the group. And as they began to realise that the noise they were hearing was gunfire, a shade of sobriety coloured the atmosphere. They had never before heard such a continuous firing of guns.

'Gentlemen——' The Major held up one hand. 'We are alerted—three Flights—for a patrol at dawn. Take-off will be at 4 a.m. As you can hear, something big is afoot, and it looks as though we'll be expected to make our contribution. You'll be called at three-fifteen. Meanwhile, will Flight Commanders please come to my office now?'

The party was over. But the one about to begin looked like being much more fun.

Frank was awake when Smithers came into the hut just after three in the morning, carrying a tray of tea-cups and attempting to wake everybody as cheerfully as possible.

'All right, Smithers, put the tray down,' said Frank. 'I'll get the others up.'

'Thank you, sir——'

The words were hardly out of the batman's mouth when the entire hut seemed to rock and they were deafened by the most almighty roar anyone there had ever heard. Delaney had moved into Frank's hut—the fourth man was a new chap called Mitchell—and it was Delaney who leapt out of bed at the sound of the explosion.

'What in the name of bejeezus was *that*?' he demanded.

No one there could know it at the time, but in fact they had heard the largest land-mine explosion of the war. The British, whose shelling had stopped around midnight, had signalled the commencement of their attack by blowing up the Messines Ridge.

Half an hour later the Squadron was ready for take-off. The engines had already been warmed up, so they could quickly taxi in flights towards take-off in the pre-dawn darkness. There was no wind so it was towards the gradually glowing skyline in the East that they took off; A Flight first, then Frank leading B Flight, then C.

It was in a great climbing arc to port that they rose behind their own lines, and in that light Frank was glad of the formation practice they'd been able to get in when they had been in England, for it was only possible really to format on the exhaust glare of the man in front.

At seven thousand feet A Flight led them across the lines. Beneath them the darkness was being gathered up by the new day, but as Frank looked down on the battlefield he could see almost nothing for the smoke which clung close to the torn and rutted ground.

But now, following the land-mine explosion, all the artillery on that front, all those guns that had been gathering since April, were conducting a symphony of bombardment. And as they flew east at that height Frank could feel the shells scream past them on their way to the Hun. It was a distinctly unhappy height at which to be flying, and he was glad when Hitchcock, leading A Flight—and in effect the whole Squadron—decided to climb.

Hitchcock too had probably realised that someone at Brigade had failed to realise how dangerous it was for aircraft to be flying on virtually the same trajectory as the shells. They went on up, their job being to hold Hun aircraft to their own side of the Front, presumably until the British attack had taken place.

That early patrol saw nothing. But after breakfast, on their next patrol, Delaney got an Albatros, which Frank and Crosby confirmed.

It wasn't until his third patrol of the day, when the sun was high in the south, that Frank really saw the enemy in force. He was in a strange mood when he took off on that third patrol. For now he had the feeling that they were being committed relentlessly to a battle which would go on and on until there was no one left to fight it.

More than that, there had been another letter from Sarah which he had received at lunch-time. She had wanted to know when it would be possible for him to call again at the hospital. It had been a kind letter, full of felicitations, and emphasising how glad she was that he had been able to see his people again. But in some way he read between the lines that she was trying to say something more.

He thought about it as he climbed high, towards the east and above the battle that was raging below; was she trying to tell him that she had changed her mind and was ready to marry him, after all, in spite of what her father said?

If so, why had she left it so late? Why had she waited so long? Since his return from England Frank had been haunted by memory of the night he had spent with Stevie. He had told Delaney how he felt, and Delaney had laughed at him.

What the hell was he worrying about? had been Delaney's response. He'd had a good time, hadn't he? The only thing he should be worrying about was the possibility of a visit to the M.O.—though not even Delaney thought it would be necessary.

But that wasn't the way Frank felt. He had told Sarah he loved her and by telling her he had committed his whole self, body and soul. In spite of her treatment of him he couldn't rid himself of the feeling that he had betrayed her. And when this thought came to him, to stir the fibres of the quiet rage which smouldered inside him, he knew a new kind of hell.

Beneath them it was now possible, at that time of day, to see the progress of the battle. The sun was high and bright and as Frank banked sharply to starboard when he turned into it, he could see the vast craters which had been made by the engineers. How those Huns occupying the ridge could have lived it was impossible to visualise. The Messines Ridge appeared to have been blown off the face of the earth.

They were perhaps five miles inside the Hun lines, at about fourteen thousand feet, and well up into the sun when Frank saw what he was looking for. Beneath him, on his port quarter, he could see what appeared to be half a dozen F.E.'s being attacked by a pack of Huns.

He looked to his right and then to his left to see if the others were with him. Quickly he again test-fired his guns. The others were with him; he signalled—he and Delaney would go down while Crosby and the other man protected their tails.

Frank sent his Pup screaming into a dive with Delaney close to his side. It was strange, but in that dive with the wind screaming through the wires, he seemed to be quite stationary. It was the Huns beneath who were coming up at him. People who have never flown can never believe how it is—this relativity of a tiny aircraft to all the elements around it.

At two hundred yards Frank sighted his Aldis on an Albatros. He was tempted to fire, but held it. Then, when he realised the Albatros was already firing at a more or less helpless F.E., he let go a short burst.

The Hun, immediately conscious of his vulnerability, broke off into a climbing turn to his right. Frank saw that Delaney, on his wing, had also picked the fellow, so he left him, pulled up slightly and over to port until he was heading straight at another German in head-on attack.

The Albatros was concentrating on a twisting F.E. whose gunner, standing up, was firing furiously. Frank closed. As he was doing so he was suddenly conscious of this being the classic Albert Ball attack. He held on.

Close. At less than fifty yards Frank fired and then— when for a horrible second he felt he might hit the Hun— he pulled off, up and over into a half roll. Upside down he could see his man burning. There was no point in following him down so Frank cut his throttle and pulled back on the stick until he was in a half-loop. At its nadir he opened his throttle fully again and climbed until he was standing the Pup on its tail.

For some moments it was difficult to see where they were. The tight circle, defensively very strong, of F.E.'s was still there. Away below he could see the smoking Albatros which he took to be the one he had shot down. But the Huns had gone. Perhaps they assumed that they had been duped into some kind of trap. Anyway, they were off.

There was no sign of his Flight. Frank could only see one Pup. It was lower by about three thousand feet and appeared to be trying to regain height. Frank flew around the grateful F.E.'s and then made for the other Pup. It was the fourth man's; he had no idea of the whereabouts of Delaney or Crosby.

And of Crosby he never would. Delaney crept in fifteen minutes after Frank had landed, but they never again heard of young Crosby.

So it went on for days; patrol after patrol. They were heartened to learn after some time that they had in fact been taking part in what the papers were calling the Battle of Messines, and they were also glad to know that the Army had secured a majority victory. It looked for a time as though this might at least be the break-out from the great stalemate. But that was all.

They flew on, day after day, without respite. It was when Frank scored his seventh victory that Delaney 'bought it'—or appeared to do so. They were on patrol and returning into the sun somewhere over the Comines region, when they were jumped by the Circus itself.

It was led by an all-red Albatros of a type that none of them had seen before, presumably flown by Richthofen himself. Perhaps the presence of the man upset them. Frank had to confess afterwards that it upset him.

But the advantage all belonged to Jerry. He had the height and he had come hurtling down out of the sun to shoot down two Pups before they knew what had hit them. Neither were flamers, for which Frank thanked God, but both spun out and it was difficult to tell whether or not they were casualties.

In seconds the whole sky was a circus. Frank tightened his Pup in a turn until he felt as though he might pull it apart, in order to get in a burst at one of the Hun, whose Albatros was painted a bright yellow. The Hun spun out, but Frank doubted if he had been seriously damaged.

Richthofen—if indeed it had been him—didn't stop. That was not his style. He had struck the Pups on his way home and that was enough. In seconds almost the sky was clear of the enemy.

At Base, half an hour later, it was decided that Delaney was missing; with one other man—a youngster who had only arrived three days before.

Delaney—Frank couldn't believe it. All that life and vitality, dead! It was unthinkable. Throughout the evening he allowed himself to sink into a despair he had not known before, deeper than any former depression he had ever experienced. It all seemed so inevitable. Days before there had been young Crosby, full of boyish enthusiasm, seeming more like a younger brother to both Frank and Delaney. And now both were gone.

Frank was sitting alone in the Mess when Major Simpson came up to him.

'Sorry about your friend, Frank,' he said. 'He . . . was a

damned good chap.'

Frank looked up from the chair in which he was deeply embedded. He held a glassful of whisky loosely in his right hand. He made no attempt to stand, not out of disrespect to Major Simpson, but because there was in him a deep protest at the whole sickening business.

'I'm s-sick of it all,' Frank said. He spoke quietly, almost viciously, with a deep anger aimed at he didn't quite know what.

'There's still time,' the Major said. 'There's still time. I wouldn't take it as being too final yet. You know Delaney better than I do. He has a tendency to bounce back.'

It was two days before Delaney 'bounced back'—not to the Squadron, but through information that he had been picked up wounded and taken to some forward hospital. Frank had just returned from his last patrol of the day when he heard the news.

It was a curiously peaceful summer evening. The weather was fine, and the whole earth seemed to be pleased that after all the heat of a long day, it could settle to rest. Frank came into the circuit, and partly because of the pleasure he found in flying through that calm evening, he allowed the others to go in first.

At fifteen hundred feet, and quite far back from the field, he cut his engine. The Pup was docile as a lamb. Full stick to port, top rudder. Check when she dropped, very gracefully. Then the alternative. Right rudder; hold top left. She was down and over the fence like a bird.

Beneath the grease which smeared his face, Frank was smiling. This time, because of all the beauty of that summer evening, he would kiss the earth with his Pup. He held off : steady. A little back pressure on the stick—wait for the stall, not too quickly . . . He held it, and then felt her touch. It was a landing worthy of the evening.

When he taxi-ed up, the ubiquitous Sergeant McFee was there, waiting and grinning.

'That was a beauty, sir,' he said. 'As fine a landing as I've ever seen you make.'

Frank wasn't so much tired as filled with a rather pleasant resignation. He pulled off his helmet while still in the cockpit, then slowly extricated himself and climbed down to slap his old friend on the shoulder. At least there was still McFee!

'Thank you, Mac. That was what I intended it to be.'

'Oh, sir——'

'Yes?'

'There's word of your friend, Mr. Delaney.'

'Delaney!' Frank's heart missed a beat. 'What about him?'

'It seems he isn't dead sir—only wounded. He's been taken to the hospital at St. Marie-Cappel. That's no' very far away, sir. Maybe you and me, if you like, could get some transport and nip over there tomorrow if you can manage it, sir.'

Manage it! In his gladness and relief Frank felt he could have walked every foot of the way. Instead he said: 'Can *you* get some transport, Mac?' He knew that the Sergeant had more influence in this direction than any mere Captain.

'Yes, sir. I think I can manage that. Just you let me know when you want to go.'

It *was* a beautiful evening, thought Frank.

Next morning Sergeant McFee and Frank made their way in a motor-cycle and sidecar along roads that were heavy with traffic on its way up to support the victory of the past days. They bounced along rutted roads, getting themselves lost repeatedly until at last they found the main road to Hazebrouck. There Frank insisted they stop for a drink, in spite of his eagerness to see Delaney.

McFee looked at the bottle of Scotch which Frank had bought. He looked at it for a long time, then he said: 'You know what the favourite drink is in my country, sir?'

'What's that, Mac?'

'No' this beer, sir—especially not French beer.' He indicated the contents of the glass he held. 'Our favourite drink is a nice glass o' whisky *chased* by a beer.'

Frank looked at the bottle he held.

'Mac, this is for Delaney—he's entitled to the first drink from it. But I'll bring some of it back for you—that's a promise.'

McFee grinned. 'Fair enough, sir. Drink his health for me while you're about it, will you?'

Sarah came when Frank asked for her. She had heard him speak of Delaney and knew that he had come to see his friend.

'Frank . . .' She held out her hand then something in his face caused her to throw herself against him. 'Oh Frank, are you all right?' she asked.

'A little tired,' he said. 'I got your letter, Sarah——'

She took hold of his hand and led him along a corridor. Her eyes were very bright and there was a warm, soft colour in her cheeks.

'Come, let's see your friend,' she said.

A much-bandaged Delaney was sitting up in bed when Frank entered the ward. He stared at Frank open-mouthed for a moment.

'Well I'll be goddamned if it isn't the Flying Ace himself!'

They laughed and Frank went forward to grip Delaney's hand, or as much as he could see of it beneath the white bandages.

Delaney's eyes were on the bottle. 'Is that . . . ?' he asked hopefully.

'It is,' said Frank. 'I thought you might just fancy a noggin.'

'My friend, you're not only an ace, you're a genius, a mind-reader,' said Delaney. He looked at Sarah. 'Fetch some glasses, girl—two glasses and a bucket. The bucket's for me.'

Sarah looked back over her shoulder at Frank as she moved away, and something in her expression caused his heart to give a quick leap. He looked down at the bandaged figure on the bed and smiled.

All things considered, he thought, it wasn't such a bad old war, after all.

THE END

A SELECTION OF FINE READING AVAILABLE IN CORGI BOOKS

Novels

☐ 552 07763 1	ANOTHER COUNTRY	*James Baldwin* 5/–
☐ 552 07938 3	THE NAKED LUNCH	*William Burroughs* 7/6
☐ 552 07317 2	THE CHINESE ROOM	*Vivian Connell* 5/–
☐ 552 08251 1	KATE HANNIGAN	*Catherine Cookson* 5/–
☐ 552 08108 6	HOLD MY HAND I'M DYING	*John Gordon Davis* 7/6
☐ 552 07777 1	THE WAR BABIES	*Gwen Davis* 5/–
☐ 552 08183 3	BOYS AND GIRLS TOGETHER	*William Goldman* 7/6
☐ 552 07968 5	THE WELL OF LONELINESS	*Radclyffe Hall* 7/6
☐ 552 08256 2	MEN THEY CAME	*Donald Hardcastle* 5/–
☐ 552 08125 6	CATCH-22	*Joseph Heller* 7/–
☐ 552 07913 5	MOTHERS AND DAUGHTERS	*Evan Hunter* 6/–
☐ 552 08252 X	HESTER ROON	*Norah Lofts* 6/–
☐ 552 08185 X	THE TOWN HOUSE	*Norah Lofts* 6/–
☐ 552 08253 8	THE BREAKING STRAIN	*John Masters* 5/–
☐ 552 08002 0	MY SISTER. MY BRIDE	*Edwina Mark* 5/–
☐ 552 08164 7	ALL SAUCE FOR THE GANDER	*Nan Maynard* 5/–
☐ 552 08092 6	THINKING GIRL	*Norma Meacock* 5/–
☐ 552 07594 9	HAWAII (colour illustrations)	*James A. Michener* 10/6
☐ 552 08124 8	LOLITA	*Vladimir Nabokov* 6/–
☐ 552 08254 6	BARNEY SNIP—ARTIST	*Frank Norman* 5/–
☐ 552 08218 X	WHEN FLAMINGOS FALL	*Mark Oliver* 5/–
☐ 552 07954 5	RUN FOR THE TREES	*James Rand* 7/6
☐ 552 07655 4	THE HONEY BADGER	*Robert Ruark* 7/6
☐ 552 08231 7	THE DAUGHTERS OF LONGING	*Froma Sand* 6/–
☐ 552 08234 1	THE LONELY LOVERS	*J. K. Sorensen* 7/6
☐ 552 07807 7	VALLEY OF THE DOLLS	*Jacqueline Susann* 7/6
☐ 552 08013 6	THE EXHIBITIONIST	*Henry Sutton* 7/6
☐ 552 08217 1	THE CARETAKERS	*Dariel Telfer* 7/–
☐ 552 07921 9	THE BASTARD Vol. I	*Brigitte von Tessin* 5/–
☐ 552 07922 7	THE BASTARD Vol. II	*Brigitte von Tessin* 7/6
☐ 552 07937 5	THE DETECTIVE	*Roderick Thorp* 7/6
☐ 552 08091 8	TOPAZ	*Leon Uris* 7/6
☐ 552 08073 X	THE PRACTICE	*Stanley Winchester* 7/6
☐ 552 07116 1	FOREVER AMBER Vol. I	*Kathleen Winsor* 5/–
☐ 552 07117 X	FOREVER AMBER Vol. II	*Kathleen Winsor* 5/–
☐ 552 07790 9	THE BEFORE MIDNIGHT SCHOLAR	*Li Yu* 7/6

War

☐ 552 08236 8	THE LUFTWAFFE WAR DIARIES (illus.)	*Cajus Bekker* 10/–
☐ 552 08190 6	THE ADMIRAL	*Martin Dibner* 7/6
☐ 552 08168 X	MONTE CASSINO	*Sven Hassel* 5/–
☐ 552 08159 0	THE WILLING FLESH	*Willi Heinrich* 6/–
☐ 552 08237 6	THE PAINTED BIRD	*Jerzy Kosinski* 5/–
☐ 552 08222 8	SAGITTARIUS RISING	*Cecil Lewis* 5/–
☐ 552 08221 X	GIMME THE BOATS	*J. E. Macdonnell* 5/–
☐ 552 07726 7	THE DIRTY DOZEN	*E. M. Nathanson* 7/6
☐ 552 08255 4	THE ENEMY SKY	*Peter Saxon* 4/–
☐ 552 08169 8	633 SQUADRON	*Frederick E. Smith* 5/–
☐ 552 08078 0	TREBLINKA (illustrated)	*Jean Francois Steiner* 7/6
☐ 552 08113 2	THE LONG NIGHT'S WALK	*Alan White* 4/–

Romance

☐ 552 08264 3	HIGHLAND INTERLUDE	*Lucilla Andrews* 4/–
☐ 552 08227 9	COTTAGE HOSPITAL	*Sheila Brandon* 3/6
☐ 552 08244 9	THE TEAM	*Hilary Neal* 3/6
☐ 552 08176 0	THE FAITHFUL FAILURE	*Kate Norway* 3/6

Science Fiction

☐ 552 08265 1	NEW WRITINGS IN S.F.-15	*ed. John Carnell* 4/–
☐ 552 08199 X	A FOR ANDROMEDA	*Fred Hoyle and John Elliot* 3/6
☐ 552 08245 7	THE SHRINKING MAN	*Richard Matheson* 4/–
☐ 552 07682 1	THE SHAPE OF THINGS TO COME	*H. G. Wells* 7/6
☐ 552 08198 1	ALL JUDGMENT FLED	*James White* 3/6

General

☐	552 07566 3	SEXUAL LIFE IN ENGLAND	*Dr. Ivan Bloch* 9/6
☐	552 08086 1	ENQUIRE WITHIN UPON EVERYTHING	*Reference* 7/6
☐	552 07593 0	UNMARRIED LOVE	*Dr. Eustace Chesser* 5/–
☐	552 07950 2	SEXUAL BEHAVIOUR	*Dr. Eustace Chesser* 5/–
☐	552 07996 0	THE ISLAND RACE (illustrated in colour)	*Winston S. Churchill* 30/–
☐	552 06000 3	BARBARELLA (illustrated)	*Jean Claude Forest* 30/–
☐	552 07804 2	THE BIRTH CONTROLLERS	*Peter Fryer* 7/6
☐	552 07400 4	MY LIFE AND LOVES	*Frank Harris* 12/6
☐	552 08121 3	FIVE GIRLS (illustrated)	*Sam Haskins* 21/–
☐	552 07745 3	COWBOY KATE (illustrated)	*Sam Haskins* 21/–
☐	552 01541 4	MAN AND SEX	*Kaufman and Borgeson* 5/–
☐	552 07916 2	SEXUAL RESPONSE IN WOMEN	*Drs. E. and P. Kronhausen* 9/6
☐	552 08247 3	THE HISTORY OF THE NUDE IN PHOTOGRAPHY (illustrated)	*Peter Lacey & Anthony LaRotonda* 25/–
☐	552 08120 5	ONE IN TWENTY	*Bryan Magee* 5/–
☐	552 08069 1	THE OTHER VICTORIANS	*Steven Marcus* 10/–
☐	552 08010 1	THE NAKED APE	*Desmond Morris* 5/–
☐	552 07965 0	SOHO NIGHT AND DAY (illustrated)	*Norman and Bernard* 7/6
☐	552 08105 1	BEYOND THE TENTH	*T. Lobsang Rampa* 5/–
☐	552 08228 7	WOMAN: a Biological Study	*Philip Rhodes* 5/–
☐	552 08089 6	MOVIES ON T.V.	*Steven Scheuer* 7/6
☐	552 08178 7	THE YELLOW STAR (illustrated)	*Gerhard Schoenberner* 21/–
☐	552 08266 X	SOCCER MY BATTLEFIELD (illus.)	*Nobby Stiles* 5/–
☐	552 08246 5	NORTH-WEST FRONTIER (illustrated)	*Arthur Swinson* 7/6
☐	552 08038 1	EROS DENIED (illustrated)	*Wayland Young* 7/6
☐	552 07918 9	BRUCE TEGNER'S COMPLETE BOOK OF KARATE	6/–

Westerns

☐	552 08225 2	THE GUNS OF DORKING HOLLOW	*Max Brand* 3/6
☐	552 08082 9	SUDDEN—APACHE FIGHTER	*Frederick H. Christian* 4/–
☐	552 08240 6	THE DEPUTIES	*J. T. Edson* 4/–
☐	552 08241 4	THE FORTUNE HUNTERS	*J. T. Edson* 4/–
☐	552 08242 2	TROUBLED RANGE	*J. T. Edson* 4/–
☐	552 08066 7	MACKENNA'S GOLD	*Will Henry* 3/6
☐	552 08261 9	THE LONELY MEN	*Louis L'Amour* 4/–
☐	552 08172 8	THE EMPTY LAND	*Louis L'Amour* 4/–
☐	552 07934 0	SHALAKO	*Louis L'Amour* 3/6
☐	552 08263 5	DONOVAN'S GUN	*Luke Short* 4/–

Crime

☐	552 08260 0	TRAPS NEED FRESH BAIT	*A. A. Fair* 4/–
☐	552 08224 4	DEATH ON THE MOVE	*John Creasey* 3/6
☐	552 08004 7	MADRIGAL	*John Gardner* 5/–
☐	552 08062 4	THE MONEY THAT MONEY CAN'T BUY	*James Munro* 5/–
☐	552 08239 2	DEATH ON THE TABLE	*Claire Rayner* 3/6
☐	552 08267 8	THE GIRL HUNTERS	*Mickey Spillane* 4/–
☐	552 08223 6	THE DELTA FACTOR	*Mickey Spillane* 4/–
☐	552 08257 0	THE MAN WHO KILLED HIMSELF	*Julian Symons* 4/–
☐	552 08258 9	THE BROKEN PENNY	*Julian Symons* 4/–